Kai's Secret

Mysteries at the Museum Series

By: R. L. Walker

To: Addison

Follow your creativity!

- Ms Walker

R. L. Walker

Dedicated to:

My students, family, and Chris

Without whom I would've finished months sooner

I hope that you enjoy this story which was inspired by time at an archaeological field school during college. Please leave a review on Amazon and Goodreads!

Prologue

Baking under a desert sun, trying to hide in the sand with bullets whizzing past my head and bouncing off the canyon walls was not how I pictured my summer. While I had hoped for an exciting adventure full of history, museum displays, and digging up new archaeological finds, I had seen things going a bit calmer in my mind at least. Crawling through the rust colored sand, I curled up behind a massive boulder to shield myself from the madman below. I can hear his voice echoing in the canyon, "You are just delaying the inevitable, I will find you. Come on out and I will make your death a quick one. Much quicker than your parents." His thick Russian accent made him difficult to understand. Did he just mention my parents? I perked up because my parents had long been dead.

"Yes, that's right. I know the truth about your parents, the truth that everyone has been keeping from you. If you come down, I will give you the answers that you seek," his accent getting thicker and his words seeming to drip honey.

Knowing I should not trust this brute, curiosity got the best of me and I sputtered involuntarily, "You knew my parents.?"

"I more than knew your parents, my dear. We were the best of friends until they betrayed me that is. For that they had to pay the price," he said nonchalantly. Then he yelled, "Gotcha!" I heard the bullet travel down the gun chamber and through the air coming right in my direction. What seemed like hours passed while I stared frozenly at the bullet spinning towards my head. Unable to move out of the way in my trance, I felt a force slam into me and a piercing pain at my temple.

Feeling sluggish, I felt my mind fog over. I was drifting back in time, back to the beginning of the summer. The sound of maniacal laughter was the last thing I heard as my world went black.

Chapter 1

My hands were sweating and shaking as I hastily ripped open the envelope and pulled out the letter. What was written inside could possibly change my whole summer, even my life, or perhaps the world! Well the whole world might be a bit of a stretch, but a girl can dream, can't she? Once the letter was out, I just stared at it for a minute. I was so scared of what it would say. The words on this page had the power to crush my childhood dreams or bring them to life. Whenever you come to a crossroads in your life where the pathway is already decided for you because of road construction you cannot help but wonder what would happen if the other road was open. While I had been thinking I brushed my straight dark hair away from my face.

Staring at the pressed white page I blinked my hazel eyes as my mind returned to earlier in the year, the true beginning one could argue. I was excited as I filled out my application to be a summer intern at the Smithsonian. They had started a new program accepting high school students to help inspire an interest in the past. The program was a mixture of curating artifacts already in storage, helping design new displays, and even had the possibility of going to a dig site to see how artifacts were brought in for curation in the museum. I had penned in my cover letter how I was trying to discover my own past as I had recently found out that I was adopted and had never grown up learning my Native American traditions. I was hoping that by studying the artifacts of my people, I would have a better understanding of myself. There was a lot riding on this letter.

"Oh, just read the darn thing already!" my older brother, Wyatt, exclaimed.

I jumped and replied, "How long have you been standing there?"

"Long enough… Do I need to read it for you? The rest of us are just as anxious to find out as you are, Kai," stated Wyatt hastily.

Gathering some courage, I opened the letter and read, "Congratulations, you have been accepted into our summer internship program. Please read through the list of required items, immunizations…." I stopped reading and shouted my joy. "Ekkkk! Everyone, I got in! I'm going to Washington D.C. this summer!" I shouted as I ran downstairs to tell my parents. "Congrats, honey," whispered my mom as she enveloped me a warm hug, "we will have to go shopping soon to get you a new wardrobe!"

"That's my girl! I knew you would get it! Well done!" congratulated my dad. He was always my biggest fan encouraging me to reach for the stars. Which was probably part of the reason why I even felt like I should and could apply for the position. It was great having parents that were so supportive even if they were not flesh and blood. They always say that blood is thicker than water, but love is thicker than blood sometimes. That did not mean that my blood parents did not love me, I never met them and tried not to judge their reasons for giving me up. Thankfully, I felt like I had a pretty good life. Yet, sometimes I was curious what my life would've been like had I grew up with them.

I looked into dad's bright green eyes so different from my own and smiled back, "Thanks, Dad, for always believing in me."

"Hey, you did it for yourself. You applied, you did the hard work in school, you wrote the letter. If you want to thank someone, thank yourself for your drive. I am so proud of you, but enough of this business. Let's go out to eat to celebrate!"

As the car pulled into my favorite restaurant, I opened my car door and stepped out into the spring rain. Everyone had survived my driving. Wyatt got out of the back seat and walked around the SUV judging my parking skills and said, "Not too bad sis, but a little close to the curb." I laughed as I dodged the puddles, skipping my way inside. Brothers, what can you do.

As I went to walk into the diner, something caught my eye. I looked over my shoulder and saw a falcon sitting on a fence post on the edge of the parking lot. It seemed like an odd place for a bird to hang out. Right at that moment the falcon turned its eyes towards me and appeared to wink before it flew off into the rain store. Shaking my head, I continued to walk inside and noticed my mom was watching me closely. I waited for her to say something about the falcon, but instead she quickly looked away and went inside. That was odd as she loved birds and had to have seen the falcon. "Hey silly, let's go! Aren't you hungry?" my brother's comment jarred me from my thoughts and I went inside.

Upon entering the familiar smell of smoked ribs lingered in the air. This place had the best ribs and the scent made my mouth water just thinking about the juicy smoky taste with a sweet and spicy flavor. The hostess smiled and led us to a table so I could happily order my favorite food. The rest of my family knew what they wanted as well and the server, Jane, knew our order, but asked, "You all want the usual?" We all nodded in agreement and she smiled back, "Great, I'll get that out quickly for you guys. Is tonight something special? Everyone seems excited or something."

My brother beamed and spoke up, "Well Kai here, just got an internship at the Smithsonian for the summer."

"Oh my stars! How exciting, Kai! You will have to tell us all about your adventures in the big city when you get back! I'll make sure to bring out some apple pie to celebrate!"

The table looked like a massacre had happened, there were bones scattered about, and used gooey wet napkins strewn about indicating that the meal was good and gone. My brother looked up from his pile of neatly stacked rib bones and pointed at the one I had left on my plate and asked, "You done with that?"

"Psshh of course not. Hands off, bottomless pit," I replied as I hurriedly scarfed it down. Then, I waved the bone in front of him just to aggravate.

"I am going to text Aunt Margaret and tell her to hide all the food in her house because you will eat her out of house and home this summer," Wyatt teased.

"Oh Wyatt, I'm sure your Aunt Margaret knows how to make your sister earn her keep. She does run Monticello," my dad mused.

My mom laughed and replied, "I remember the time that she picked both of you up by your ears and lectured you on the importance of history. I suppose her passion must have rubbed off onto you, Kai."

"I did like when she took me to several digs on Monticello, it was beyond cool to be involved in something once in a lifetime like that. Staying at her house was like having a slumber party in a museum," I recalled fondly with a grin.

Jane came back over with the pie and to clear off some of the dishes and asked, "So when will you be leaving us?"

"Oh next week, so I have a few days to pack," I replied.

"And to shop! We need to get you outfits that are ready for the capital!" exclaimed my mom.

Both my brother and dad exhaled with an "Oomph".

"Don't worry, we are going after we drop you guys off," instructed my mom. She knew that they did not like to be out at the mall, and honestly, I did not really enjoy being around tons of people either. Yet, I knew that having some more professional outfits would be best even if trying everything in the store would be a pain.

After dropping the guys off at the house, my mother and I went on a clothing adventure. We stopped at a few outdoor gear places to get a few things to make being on an archaeological dig easier and less sweaty. Then, we stopped at several department stores to get some professional outfits and the like.

Within a few hours we were done and back in the car which looked like a hoarder had went on a buying binge. There were sacks from several different stores scattered in the backseat. I was pretty exhausted and looked around with a worried expression. My mother understood this look and simply said, "Don't worry dear, it takes up less room in a suitcase. Now let's get home and get to packing!"

"Sounds good to me! Only can we skip the packing until tomorrow?" I asked.

My mom looked thoughtful and replied, "Of course."

I started the car and drove us back home and carried in my loot. I waved at my brother and dad, then continued to carry my bags to my room. By the time I got all my bags upstairs, I collapsed on my bed and fell asleep from exhaustion.

I had just gotten a note that we were going to have a very eventful summer. My uncle wanted myself and several of his henchmen to break into the Smithsonian of all places. He did have some doozy ideas, but this one took the cake. At first, I told him it was a ridiculous idea and wouldn't go along with it. However, he mentioned that my sister was young and not yet introduced to the family business and if I wanted to keep her out of it, then I needed to play my part.

After working together to figure out the best time for the heist. It was decided that we would wait until all the summer interns showed up. Since it would be such a confusing time, no one would notice a few new people filtering in and out. Plus, we could gain access to the basement rooms where some of the more valuable and culturally significant artifacts were stored and cleaned. The thought was that if we took the artifacts, then the Navajo tribe would have no choice but to let the pipeline go through. As of now it was being held up because some lawyers claimed that it was going through sacred ground. My family had a direct stake in the success of the pipeline being built. While I was not super crazy about the idea of becoming an international criminal, I did not want to involve my sister further. My summer fate had been sealed.

Chapter 2

Tossing and turning I awoke to the sound of wings flapping. Confused I looked around the room to see if a bird or bat had gotten in. Only to my shock I was not in my room but surrounded by the empty abyss that was the dark night sky. Worried I was going to fall I started to flail around only to realize that I was going up even higher. I looked over to my left and saw that instead of an arm, I had wings! What on Earth? This couldn't be real! I looked back and forth between my wings and saw that I also had claw like feet. What madness! Eventually, I looked down and saw that the land was barely even a speck below me. Scared out of my mind, I let out a shriek and curled up into a ball. As I hurtled towards the Earth below, I saw a falcon appear to my left and catch me. Then, the falcon spoke up, "Trust your wings! Look around you."

Carefully, I opened my eyes and looked down. Very slowly I started flapping my arms and it was smooth sailing. As I looked down, I saw a group of people visiting what looked to be a grave. They were wearing the dress of my ancestors and singing and crying. Across the way I saw something else, something different. I tried to get closer to read the signs, but I could not.

All of a sudden, I woke up in a cold sweat to the sound of my heavy breathing with the morning light pouring through my windows. I started to flap my arms only to realize to my relief that were featherless and just my arms. Man, what a strange dream I thought. Sometimes, I have strange dreams, but this one seemed to top the list. Glancing at the clock, I saw that it was early and about seven. Afraid to go back to sleep, I got up to wander downstairs to get some breakfast. As I was leaving the room, I noticed something out of the corner my eye and looked over. It was a feather floating under the bed.

I quickly dashed out the door and closed it behind me. Whatever was going on in there was not something I was ready to understand. I bolted down the stairs and into the kitchen almost knocking over dad and his coffee. "Whoa there, where are you in a hurry to go this morning?" he asked.

"Uh, I was just hungry," I fibbed and snagged a bagel from the counter and put it in the toaster.

My mom was looking at me cautiously and asked, "Everything okay?"
"Oh yea, I am just excited about the summer. That's all," I mumbled. I tried to act normal and eat my breakfast, but I was feeling anything except normal. This was one of those things that you want to tell your parents but are afraid to because they might have committed or something. So, I got out my phone and looked busy texting my friends telling them the news. Many were excited and wanted to visit me in D.C. Then, I got a text from my cousin.
Johana: [Hey cuz! Heard you got the internship at the Smithsonian! Congrats!]
Kai: [Thanks! I am pretty excited!]
Johana: [If you need anything let me know! I will be in and out of D.C. this summer. I am representing the tribe in a legal battle.]
Kai: [Wow! What's going on? Way to use those lawyer skills!]
Johana: [I'll have to tell you when we meet up in D.C. I don't want to take any chances with text messages. Stay safe, talk to you later.]

Hmmm, what an odd conversation I thought. It sounded like things were getting more interesting by the day. I would just have to wait and find out though. While I had my phone out, I went ahead and booked my plane ticket to D.C. and sent a copy of the itinerary to my aunt so she would know when to pick me up. Planning my trip helped take my mind off of the previous night.

I looked over and saw my mother reading through my checklist of what to bring, where I needed to go, and all the tedious stuff that I had sort of skimmed through earlier. I could tell by the look on her face that we were going to go over it shortly. Thus, I made my way upstairs and checked off everything while packing. After I was finished, I told my mom I needed a break before we did anything else.

Walking outside, I wandered over to the treehouse in the backyard. It was a warm summer day and my favorite wildflowers were blooming under the tree. Casually, I wandered through the gardens and looked out towards the Flat Irons. It was a view that I would never tire of and one that I would miss while in the busy city. I climbed up into the treehouse and stared up at the fluffy clouds floating by in various shapes and sizes and one even looked like a ship waiting to set sail. Which seemed rather symbolic as I was about to set sail on my own adventure. Sitting up high and looking at the archaeology maps I had pinned to the wall reminded me that this had always been my dream, but I couldn't help feeling a little scared too. "Hey Kai, supper's ready!" shook me from my thoughts and I climbed down from my childhood creation preparing to step into reality.

The next few days went by in a whirlwind of activity that I could barely keep up with and before I knew it I was waving bye to my family at the airport. With my ticket in hand and bags checked, I headed through security and walked to my plane.

Chapter 3

Several hours later, I groggily walked off the plane in Washington D.C. While walking through the airport, I tried to spot my aunt, but it was very hectic. Everyone was running around trying to catch their plane or grab a cab. Well I wasn't in Kansas anymore that was for sure and I wasn't sure if I liked it. Big cities always seemed exciting, but all the people running around just was a bit overwhelming. The lines of people twisted through the corridors like a snake that was never ending.

Shouts from every possible language could be heard. Signs with "Welcome to the U.S" were around every corner even one that said, " welkom bij de VS." I had never seen that language before, but D.C. was a place full of diversity and excitement. However, at last I was able to reach it's end where I saw my aunt waving from behind security.

"Hello! Over here, Aunt Margaret!" I shouted as I waved.

She came up and wrapped me in a lavender scented bear hug and said, "Welcome back my little historian!" with her dove gray eyes sparkling. "Let's get your things and get out of here! You hungry?"

"Always!" I laughed.

Aunt Margaret replied with a cluck, "You'd never guess it by how skinny you look! You are just growing like a weed. I wish I still had that youthful metabolism."

"Is your favorite D.C. restaurant still around?" I pondered.

"Hmmm I take it that you want to go to the Pad Thai restaurant?" teased Aunt Margaret.

"Maybe…" I responded.

"Well let's grab your suitcase and get you some dinner! You have an early exciting day tomorrow!" claimed my aunt as she pulled me down to the luggage carousel.

Along the moving belt, suitcases were spit out much like a toad spits out a terrible tasting insect. I stood near where they were exiting and waited to spot my own purple roller bag. After what seemed like ages of watching black suitcases come out, I saw something colorful. As it neared me I saw that it was too big to be mine and had a skull sticker half hanging off. We watched several more duffel bags go around and around with no one claiming them, then out popped my purple bag with the peace sign making it stand out. I grabbed it off the conveyor belt quickly before it disappeared out of sight.

Rolling my bag behind me, we wound our way through the crowds and out to the taxi stand. Since my aunt lived close to her work and by the metro she did not have a car, she claimed that they used up too much of the resources she was fighting to preserve. The few times I got to ride in a cab always made me feel like I was the Queen of England. My aunt knew just where to wait to get a cab the quickest and one that would go to her area of town.

A few minutes later we were zipping through the streets and traffic headed off towards her neighborhood, Penn Quarter, which was a historic area within walking distance of The Smithsonian and several other museums. If I were to live in a city, it was the exact sort of place that I would want to be. It was not very far away from Chinatown either which made for some vibrant architecture to take in as we drove by the giant gates. Once we passed the arches covered with jade and ruby paint, I knew we were getting close.

The taxi came to a screeching halt in front of a brick covered building, and I got out while my aunt tipped the driver. It was horribly humid outside and I could feel the sweat start to bead on my brow as I struggled to pull my suitcase from the trunk. Walking up the steep stairs I was greeted by an older gentleman who nodded at my aunt and said, "Welcome back Ms. Fitzgerald".

"Thanks, Charles! This is my niece, Kai, she is visiting from Boulder, Colorado. She going to do an internship at the Smithsonian this summer. Therefore, she will be in and out of here a lot!" bragged Aunt Margaret.

Charles stuck out his hand and exclaimed, "Nice to meet you, young lady. Hope you enjoy your summer here."

"I will!" I replied as I shook his hand, "Nice to meet you, as well."

Walking over to the elevator, I was surprised it was already open and waiting for us. My aunt walked ahead and punched in the floor number, six, which was the top floor. Beethoven played in the background as I looked around the shiny interior of the elevator with its burgundy carpets. With a ping, the elevator came to a stop and the doors leapt open. I followed my aunt down the hallway lit by old fashioned lamps.

Following the flowery patterns on the carpet we continued down the dimly lit hallway when we heard a door creak closed. I jumped as my aunt placed a reassuring hand on my shoulder. "Don't worry, that's just the meddling woman down the hall, Katya. She likes to think of herself as the neighborhood watch. It's a safe building," murmured her aunt.

Easing around me, Aunt Margaret took the key from her pocket and twisted the key to open the heavy wooden door with a magnolia stained glass window. "Welcome to the Magnolia apartment. I'm lucky enough to overlook the central garden and have a view of the famous magnolia tree," explained my aunt. The heavy door swung open almost inviting me with the flower blossom glass smiling back at me. Behind me I could hear my aunt's heels clicking on the polished wood floors. I moved from the foyer to the living area with my mouth open in awe. My aunt clucked, "Don't worry, these furnishings have survived for over a century so they can keep until morning to explore more."

I followed the "click, click" of her shoes as she led me down the hall to my bedroom. "Feel free to freshen up a bit. I ordered some takeout Thai, but it won't be here for at least thirty minutes," instructed Aunt Margaret.

"Great! I will put my stuff away and be right out!" I called as I put my suitcase up on a chair to start unpacking.

"Creak!" I heard as the door swung closed behind me as my aunt left the room. I began to unpack my internship clothes and hung them up in the armoire, then I placed my everyday jeans and t-shirts in the dresser. Near the door, I laid out some of my nicer flats and a pair of hiking boots just in case we went on an adventure. As I was pulling out my clothes, I saw an odd dark striped feather float out and onto the floor. We didn't have a bird and I was not in the habit of collecting feathers, so I bent down to pick it up. Examining it closely, I saw that it was soft to the touch and seemed to be newly mottled. It was amazing that it survived being shoved in my bags and wasn't bent or broke. I wonder where it came from.

"Ding dong", the sound of the doorbell jarred me from my thoughts, I absentmindedly set the feather off to the side by the lamp. Figuring that the food had arrived, I walked down the hall to greet my aunt as the spicy aroma wafted into the room. My stomach growled indicating that it too had noticed the food. As I neared the kitchen, I saw my aunt give the delivery man a tip and bring the food in. We were both so hungry that we quickly got out the chopsticks and dug into our meals.

Leaning back from the table with a full stomach, I said, "Thanks for ordering in my favorite place. I think I am too exhausted to do much else now."

"You don't want to go on the walking tour tonight?" my aunt amusingly pondered. My eyes widened in surprise which prompted my aunt to say, "Don't worry. I am a bit tired as well. Plus, you have a big day tomorrow. We have the whole summer to explore the city."

Nodding, I got up and gave my aunt a kiss on the cheek and went back to my room. As I drifted off to sleep I hoped that my dreams from the previous night did not return.

Chapter 4

Running from the visitor's desk to the basement, I worried I would be late for my first day as an intern. "What if I am the only one who got the location mixed up?" I thought. I could barely hear the sound of my feet over the pounding of my heart. Trying not to trip, I hurried down the stairs. Door names blurred by in my frantic search, heading towards the end of the hall marked by two heavy wood doors. When I reached my destination, I slowed down, caught my breath, and walked in hoping no one would notice.

With the creak of the door, every head in the auditorium swung towards me and my slightly dramatic entrance. I smoothed my black skirt and tried to take a seat in the back when the door flew open behind me. "Sorry, I'm late guys," shouted a girl with hair that looked like it had been through a hurricane. She tripped and her books flew in every possible direction.

I was thinking, "Thank goodness, I didn't do that," when the auditorium erupted with laughter. I wanted to help the girl, but also wanted to distance myself so I wouldn't get in trouble as well. I handed her the books at my feet and quickly took a seat. I could see her face turn red with humiliation like the temperature rising in a thermometer.

The director spoke up with a sarcastic tone, "So glad that you could join us, finally." She continued on telling us what our summer internships would require, the rules, the expectations, and how much we were already disappointing her. Her nasally voice and dark beady eyes just made me squirm even more in my seat.

The boy next to me leaned over and whispered, "Don't worry her bark is worse than her bite."

"Well I don't want to find out! Hopefully, she won't remember my late entrance. They didn't tell us that it was down here, I went to the visitor's desk. I had no idea this place was this enormous!" I frantically whispered back.

Once we had all our information, they told us to follow the schedule that was handed to us and go to our rooms. I pulled out my schedule from my bag and tried to figure out where to go. As I was intently studying the paper, the boy who I had sat beside smiled and stated, "Room 045 is right down the hall, I can walk you there if you'd like."

"How do you know all this stuff? Maybe I'm just an idiot who can't figure out how to navigate a building," I murmured in an exasperated tone.

"Technically, I am in charge of the summer interns as I am a yearlong intern and studying museum management, but also because I have already been in your shoes. If it helps I sat in the front row and asked a question. Which put me on the director's bad side for a quick minute, but I recovered and so will you," remarked the boy.

Someone bumped into me from behind and I saw a girl with glamorous dark looks giving me a glare. Wondering what I did to deserve her scorn, the boy took my arm and steered me in the correct direction. "You are supposed to be working with the Navajo collection correct? It's this way," stated the boy, "By the way I'm Alex."

"How did you know where I was interning? You don't have all the interns memorized, do you? If so that is really creepy," I stated flatly.

"I spend some time memorizing the names of the interns I am in charge of and it just so happens that my area of interest is in the Navajo collection," replied Alex.

"You aren't just a student?" I stuttered. Wondering how I managed to make two enemies already in the same day.

Alex slyly grinned while he joked, "Don't worry I won't hold it against you."

When we arrived at the Navajo collection room, he opened the door and allowed me to pass first. I saw that there were a few dark lab tables with packets and name tags. I walked over and found my name. I leafed through the packet and saw that their handouts showing up how to do various types of archaeological museum displays, how to label artifacts, how to set them up, and more. Each table had a small set of artifacts in the middle with several labels. I carefully touched the shard of pottery marveling at the smooth glaze and detailed painted design.

I felt a tap on my shoulder and flinched. It was the girl sitting next to me, she smiled then pointed up front. I saw that Alex was standing and waiting on the interns to pay attention. Gently, I laid down the artifacts and sat up straight. He smoothed his ruffled blonde hair out of his face and smiled broadly welcoming everyone to the internship and began explaining what all we would be doing. Once he told us about the expectations, he began to flip through the packet explaining how to catalogue items, label them, and properly clean them. Lifting a piece of pottery, he inquired, "Can anyone tell me how you can tell the difference between the inside and outside of this shard?"

Quickly, I raised my hand. Alex pointed at me, his deep cobalt blue eyes seeming to sear into mine. I responded, "The outside is fired and glazed feeling smooth, while the inside is rough and tends to look like sandstone and unfinished."

Alex looked impressed and acknowledged, "Very good, Kai. At least someone is paying attention to my rambling."

Hearing some snickers, he continued with his lecture and asking us questions. After what seemed like a few minutes, he looked at his watch and stated, "Alright, it's lunch time. The cafeteria is on the main floor and I recommend the turkey bacon wrap and advise you to avoid the chicken salad. See you back here at one o'clock sharp."

Wow, time really flew by this morning. As I got up, I noticed the girl who had bumped into me earlier and gave her a glare back. After which, the girl beside me whispered, "Don't worry about her. I'm Anna, you want to grab lunch with me?"

"Sure! Do you know her? She seems to hate me for no reason," I murmured.

Anna rolled her violet eyes and tossed her dark curls from her face and giggled, "Oh that's Luna the Looney as we call her behind her back. She thinks because her dad is a chief of some tribe that she should automatically get to work with the Navajo collection. Some of us have been applying for years. I am a freshman in college and finally got in."

"Do you go to school with her?" I wondered aloud.

Anna shook her head and replied, "No, we just met her today, but the little we talked to her at breakfast was enough. Let's go, I'll introduce you to the group of girls."

I followed Anna up to the cafeteria but found it odd that this new girl hated me and that Anna was so quick to judge. This was all pretty foreign to me as all the girls I went to school with I had known since birth practically and we all got along. I wasn't sure I was going to like the politics of Washington.

I followed Anna up the stairs to the cafeteria where her friends were all sitting. Most wore business like skirt suits looking almost like they had uniforms on. I noticed that they were all eating the same thing; a turkey bacon wrap. I couldn't help but wonder if the girls were clones of one another or if the only good food was in fact the turkey bacon wrap. Several of the girls did not look up when Anna introduced me, but one girl did peak over top of her glasses seeming to measure me up in one long sweep of her gaze.

I waved and smiled at the girls, then said, "Well I need to go grab some lunch see you in a bit." Walking over to the cafeteria line, I looked around to see what looked or smelled good. The chicken salad had a distinct odor to it, so I avoided it. Having no particular aromas stand out to me, I grabbed a salad with chicken and an apple, then continued through the line to pay.

Sitting down, I saw the girls look at my lunch selection and sneer. Anna spoke up, "I should have told you we eat turkey on Mondays. Next time you won't make that same mistake."

"Oh, I've never eaten a particular meal on the same day. Our school in Boulder has a rotating fresh menu so I am just used to doing everything differently. Sorry, didn't mean to offend you girls," I added, holding my ground.

Snort! I heard some muffled giggling behind me and turned to see it was the girl from earlier. In place of her dower expression earlier, she met my eyes and smiled. I pondered why she would think this was funny, but it seemed like I had gained an ally.

Anna ignored the interaction and said, "I can't wait til after lunch, they let us work in artifact storage on our first day by ourselves!"

Chapter 5

Kaboom! I heard loud sound echo in the artifact storage basement. A little unnerved, I was contemplating going to investigate the matter when I heard a door click closed. A slight panic sat in as I wondered if someone had just left or came in. I had thought I was alone in this section, so I gathered my courage and went for a walk.

Inching my way through the aisle of dusty boxes like a fox sneaking up on its prey. The musty smell of old dust filled my nostrils, the kind that you find at your grandmother's house. Craning my neck, I couldn't see over the boxes, so I made my way through the maze until I reached the end. A box was knocked over in the middle of the room, the artifacts inside had scattered all over the dirty floor. Looking up I saw where it had originally set and instinctively knew that it had not mysteriously fallen on its own.

For a moment I froze, I knew that I should tell someone, but I wasn't sure if I should run out, wait, call someone, scream, or hide in case someone or something was still lurking in the shadows. As the minutes seemed to tick by inside my head, I heard footsteps coming from the corridor, and impulsively shouted, "Hey! I'm in here. I think there has been a break in!"

Creaaaak... The door swung open and Alex stepped into the room. He called out to find where I was hidden in the rows of artifacts. I waved and stepped out into the open so that he could see where I was. I showed him the box and explained, "I heard a crash, then the creak of the door opening. I am pretty sure whoever broke in here has escaped. We need to tell someone about this!"

Alex looked around very serious, then whispered, "So you saw it..."

"Saw what?" I asked.

He looked around the room again making sure there was no one to hear him and he said, "The minotaur..."

"You don't seriously think I am going to believe that story, do you?" I sneered.

Alex shrugged and stated flatly, "Believe me or not. It's your choice, but he lurks down here sometimes. They accidentally opened a box from Greece, a present from the president, and out ran the Minotaur. He has been wreaking havoc in the artifact storage room ever since."

With that he walked out of the room quietly, leaving me alone and apprehensive about what I had learned. Thankfully, it was close to the end of the day so I cleaned up the artifacts and put the sorted mess back where it belonged. My hands were shaking as I placed the labels on the pieces and situated them in the storage containers. Once I was convinced that everything was in its correct place. I calmly made my way to the doors, unsure if there was a creature or person looking about the room. Either way I did not want to find out.

Making it to the door, I pulled on the handle and swore I heard heavy breathing behind me. The hairs on my neck stood up like stray dog about to be cornered. I turned around yet saw nothing behind me. Trying to convince myself it was all in my head, I quickly walked through the door and scampered down passageway to the elevator.

I rapidly pushed the elevator button, like tapping it faster would somehow make the doors open quicker. Ding! The doors opened and I scampered inside, where I kept hitting the door close button. As the doors were closing I swore I saw a bull like man running down the hallway, and right as the doors an angry face with horns came changing. Clunk! The sound vibrated off the doors and the elevator lurched into motion bringing me up from the basement. I fell back against the elevator in relief.

As I chased her into the elevator I was worried, "What if she stops running and confronts me?" I'll be forced to hurt her or she could possibly see through this ridiculous disguise. I'm not sure whose idea it was to use a mythical beast to try to scare Kai off, but it certainly was not mine. Why I even went along with it I'm not sure. All I knew was that I didn't want her finding out our business. My whole family would be ruined and penniless which would be beyond appalling.

The door closed on her horrified face and I felt a sense of elation and remorse battling within me. I truly hated scaring her, but I was glad she had run. Personally, I had figured her to be too proud to run from a costume. Maybe she wasn't as bright as we had feared. Perhaps she would not stumble onto our plan.

I decided to ram the door for good measure. May as well give her a real scare. That might terrorize her into leaving things alone.

Coming to a stop, the elevator doors popped open and I walked out trying to act normal. Apparently, I was not able to mask my fear because the dark haired girl from earlier walked up and asked, " Hey! Are you okay? You look a little worried. That creep didn't do anything to you did he?"

"What creep?" I inquired wondering if she somehow knew about my experience in the basement.

"Alex. I never did like him, gives me goose bumps and not in a good way," the girl commented, "by the way my name is Lina."

I smiled back and offered my name, and pondered, "Hmm I didn't get that vibe, but my brother says I am too trusting." Then I asked, "Why do those other girls not like you?"

"Your guess is as good as mine. I'm not here to make friends, but to help my people preserve our heritage. Being trained as an archaeologist and museum curator will give me the power to tell the world about the Navajo and all the great things that we have accomplished. Do you see how much of our history just sits in boxes? Back home things are really bad and maybe by exposing people to our history, I can make reservation life better," informed Lina.

"I'm Navajo, too!" I exclaimed excited about our shared heritage that I was hoping to learn more about.

Lina looked me up and down and noted, "You don't look Navajo. Your eyes are hazel and look more like the forests than the sands of the desert."

"My mother was Navajo and my father was not. Apparently, they met while he was in Peace Corps teaching on the reservation," I began, "I am trying to learn more about my mother's heritage. Which is why I applied to the program."

"Was?" Lina asked.

I mumbled softly, "My parents died when I was very young, I don't really remember them. My aunt and uncle raised me."

Lina's grew soft with understanding, "I'm sorry. My mother died when I was little as well. Maybe we aren't as different as I thought."

Grinning I suggested, "Let's grab lunch together!"

Lina nodded her agreement and said, "Sounds like a plan, I need to get going though. Don't want to catch the bus in the dark."

Waving goodbye, I continued down the hall and walked out to the main visitor's area. Reaching the revolving doors, I squinted my eyes as I stepped out into the bright sunlight. Being in the basement all day had heightened my night vision, but it took my eyes a minute to adjust.

After looking down at the concrete sidewalk for several seconds, I lifted my face and breathed in the smell of fresh air. Spinning in a circle I turned back to look at the Smithsonian's entrance. It looked almost like part of history with its stoic appearance. This time of night people were not running in and out like they usually were and it appeared to be taking a nap.

With a final glance, I closed the chapter on my first day. Which was more eventful than I had anticipated? Strolling over to the light, I hit the button for the pedestrian crossing and waited patiently for the walk sign to flash. Cars were buzzing by quick enough to blow my chestnut hair into my face. I pulled my ear buds out of my purse and turned on my favorite Beatles tunes, jamming away. Suddenly, the light turned to the white person walking, so I started to cross the street.

Beep! Beep! The honking of a horn and screeching of tires caused me to stop in my tracks and look up. My eyes widened when I saw how close the truck gate was to my face. The angry driver shook his fist at me, while the others in the crosswalk shouted a few choice words back and pointed at our walk sign. Standing frozen in shock, I didn't move until someone from behind me told me, "Hurry up before the light changes and you really do get hit."

Making it to the other side, I was glad that the rest of my walk to my aunt's apartment did not include any more street crossings. In Boulder, no one would ever come close to hitting a pedestrian, let alone honk and scream obscenities at them. Hurriedly, I swiftly walked the last few blocks to my aunt's anxious to be inside and done with a crazy first day as an intern.

As I made it to the entrance to the building, Charles asked, "Your aunt just arrived a few moments ago. You have a pleasant first day Kai?"

Surprised, I stuttered, "Uh it was okay for a first day, I suppose. If you count being chased by Minotaurs, going to the wrong room, and almost getting hit by a car pleasant, then I guess so."

"Be careful crossing those streets, the drivers in D.C. are as crazy as the politicians," replied Charles.

I laughed and he rang the elevator button for me. Waving bye, I entered as the doors opened trying to decide how much I should tell my aunt.

From the living room I heard, "How was your first day? Come in here, let's celebrate." So, I walked in to see my aunt sipping a club soda while leafing through a travel magazine, anxiously awaiting news about my day. I was bursting at the seams to tell someone, anyone, what I had seen today, but at the same time I was worried about that my aunt would just send me home. I mean who wants to watch their crazy niece for the summer?

Carefully, I began, "Well it didn't start out near as well as I had hoped."

"Oh, why is that Kai?" Aunt Margaret wondered with a small frown furrowing her brow.

"For starters I went to the wrong room so I wound up walking in late. Then, it wasn't even quiet, everyone saw me walk in late. I was so embarrassed," I grimaced at my own humiliation. Somehow in the retelling, it seemed even worse.

My aunt held up a hand and blurted, "Say no more, sometimes first days are learning experiences. How about we put it behind us by going for a walk and getting some frozen yogurt? I didn't have a pleasant day either."

I perked up at the mention of ice cream, albeit a healthier version, and exclaimed, "What a great idea!"

Chapter 6

With a new day and a fresh start, I was ready for anything. Walking back to the Smithsonian, I noticed that there was a huge crowd along the sidewalk which was odd this early. I hoped that they would not interrupt my walk too much. As I got closer, I saw that they were waving signs and shouting on the mega phone about stopping a pipeline and how Washington was violating local rights. Trying not to get involved I scurried through the crowd, the best I could. Once I reached the entrance I ducked inside and the click of the door made me feel instantly safer.

Trying not to dawdle, I scurried to the main classroom determined not to be late today. Which thankfully, I wasn't so I settled in for the lecture series. After another new lesson from the curator, we broke off into groups again for the morning. Anna joined me on the walk down the stairs and asked, "So did you enjoy your second night in D.C.? It's a great place to party if you know the right people."

"My aunt showed me around and we got some frozen yogurt at the new hipster hangout. People watching there was out of this world, plus they have all kinds of weird flavors, such as artisan dill pickle yogurt of all things," I marveled, "How about you?"

"The girls and I strolled around downtown and we even snuck in to a club! I'm sure that's not something new for you. If you want a fake I.D. we can find a way to get you one," Anna challenged.

I thought for a moment, then remarked, "Thanks, but my aunt really doesn't want me wandering off without her in the city. I don't want to get sent back home and mess up my internship."

Anna sniffed and walked away about the same time that Alex praised in a muffled whisper, "Way to sidestep the trouble. Archaeology is way more exciting than her dad's country club."

"Aren't you not supposed to say those things about students?" I snorted.

"Technically, she's not my student. However, forgive my lapse of judgement. I just wanted to look out for one of my current students and make sure that she was not falling in with the wrong crowd," Alex coaxed.

Rolling my eyes, I tried to cover up the blush rising up my cheeks. Thinking to myself, "He *probably says that to all the interns. Stay focused.*" Brushing by him, I went in to class to start our lesson on setting up exhibit displays.

After several hours of meticulous note taking, we were allowed to practice making our own displays. Alex starting grouping people together and assigning them box numbers. Which they would go to the basement, find, and bring back up to assemble. I heard Alex call my name followed by Lina's name. Our eyes met across the room and we smiled. She came over to where I was sitting and offered to go with me to the basement. Somehow, she must have sensed that whatever was bothering me yesterday, started in the basement.

We walked out the door and took the stairs rather than the elevator as Lina claimed not to trust them. My stomach leapt to my throat like a jaguar as the elevator creaked and sighed on its way down the shaft when it finally came to a thudding halt. The letter B lit up red and the doors whooshed open. Lina sensing my hesitation led the way and motioned that it was safe to follow her. Her brow furrowed together and confusion fogged her eyes when I still did not exit the elevator standing as stiff as a statue. Lina gently called, "Hey there are no zombies down here, we need to get our supplies."

I croaked, "Not zombies, but minotaurs."

"Oh you are just listening to stories and being ridiculous. Let's go." Lina placed a surprisingly firm hand on my arm and tugged me out as the doors closed leaving us trapped in the basement. Slowly, my feet seemed to start moving on their own accord and I realized that the minotaur had not leaped out and devoured us yet so I must have imagined yesterday's events. Strange things had been happening to me lately so who knows what sort of psychosis I had put myself in.

Walking through the maze of dusty shelves, I did not notice any disturbances and no signs of a minotaur. No scuffle marks, no tufts of brown hair, no signs of life at least not anything that had been alive in the last century. Passing boxes full of European contact artifacts, we realized that we were in the wrong section, and brushed by our classmates leaving with their box of artifacts. One of them snickered under their breath, "We're going to win the contest. Good luck finding your box," as they ran back to the elevator.

I looked over and met Lina's determined onyx gaze and knew that we weren't going to be stopped by a few pests. Lina tossed her long black hair and squared her shoulders like she was going to battle and huffed, "Let's show them what we are made of." She took off down the aisles quickly scanning for our time period and before I knew it she was out of sight.

A fog of uneasiness drifted over me as I tried to keep up with where she went, but I couldn't see a trace of her. Silence blanketed the storage room, almost seeming like there was not a trace of Lina left. Feeling frantic I screamed, "Lina!"

"What's wrong with you? I'm right here! You sure are a jumpy one. You watch too many of those crime and horror shows?" Lina exclaimed with one dark eyebrow delicately arched.

I breathed a sigh of relief and shrugged my shoulders hoping to change the subject. "So, what have you got in that box?" I asked while trying to peek under the lid. Lina shifted the box so that I could see the label on the side. I saw, "**Navajo-box 232**". Wondering what could be inside, I peeked under the box and Lina closed it on my fingers. Yelping, I jumped back and stared at her in shock.

"Silly, we need to look together. It's not fair, if you get a head start on identifying the artifacts," Lina clucked with a smirk.

"Caught me," I joked trying to look innocent. I didn't want Lina to think I was afraid of my own shadow or anything since I had secretly been worried that there was a minotaur head in the box. I really needed to stop with these flights of fancy or horror in this case. Clearly Lina did not have any fears and I shouldn't listen to some silly intern telling ghost stories to the newbie. Shaking my head to clear it, I decided right then and there to stop letting fear ruin my experience.

With a spring to my step marking my new outlook on this project, I led the way and opened the door for Lina. We were going to work in a small room in the basement so there was no need to go back on the elevator. Several other groups passed us going to get boxes and going to their assigned room. Arriving at 007, I paused and looked in. Lina continued past me and set the box on the table, while I closed the door and turned on the light. It came on with a low hum as the bulb flickered. Watching as if in a trance, I saw it blink, then stop, and blink some more, appearing to be communicating with me. Catching Lina giving me a strange look, I gave the light one last look, then made my way over to the table. "Let's take a look at what we have here," I began as I lifted the lid. I shut my eyes tight and waited to hear Lina scream when she saw something horrid. When I heard nothing, I peaked in the box with one eye. In shock, I opened both eyes and stared, then looked at Lina who was also staring blankly at the empty box.

"Where are the artifacts?" wondered Lina.

I looked in, under, and around the box, yet there was no sign of the artifacts. "Maybe we grabbed the wrong box," I offered as a suggestion.

"No, this one matches the one on the list," uttered Lina, "See, it says right here. Perhaps you are right and something fishy is going on. Artifacts shouldn't go missing, we just spent all the time learning how everything has to be catalogued."

"You're right. We should go show the director immediately. Perhaps someone mixed up the boxes, or there is a thief wandering freely around," I blurted.

Lina's eyebrows scrunched together like a caterpillar as she grew serious, "What if they blame us? We should just return the box, then we won't get in trouble."

"Why would we get in trouble? We didn't do anything wrong. They need to catch this person so nothing else goes missing," I stated. I could hear my father's voice quoting Thomas Jefferson to me, "He who permits himself to tell a lie once, finds it much easier to do it the second time." Lying was not looked upon fondly in my family and I was not about to start now that they were thousands of miles away.

"Hmmmp. You can tell you did not grow up on the reservation. If anything, ever went missing in town, the reservation was the first place the sheriff always looked. Even though we were always the ones having our land stolen. You can tell if you want, but I don't want to go with you," Lina snapped.

Chapter 7

"Ugh, irresponsible interns!" exclaimed the director with her icy blue eyes boring holes through me, "It would be nice if they could actually send me someone competent for once."

"But ma'am.." I stammered.

"No, buts! Those are the worst excuses anyways. Off you go! Find out where you misplaced those artifacts before I send you packing!" hissed the director. She made a shoo shoo motion with her bony hands as her nails clicked away at the keyboard muttering about disorganized kids.

Instantly, I felt my back stiffen and I turned on my heel and marched back down to the room Lina had elected to stay in. The whole way down the hall I tried to keep my composure, but inside I was fuming. I burst into the room and said, "She didn't even listen to me!"

"Well don't say I didn't warn you. What are you so surprised about? You know no one ever believes a kid," Lina scolded with a frown.

"Not where I come from. I am just going to work hard and prove her wrong. Someone is stealing from the museum and I am going to prove it," I vowed, "I have always worked hard and never felt unvalued before."

Lina looked at me skeptically, still trying to decide what to make of me I'm sure when she added, "Count me in. Where should we start?"

I thought for a moment trying to figure out what our next step should be. We were budding archaeologist or detectives of the past. If we looked for clues to figure out how ancient societies worked, what would keep us from searching for clues to see who stole the artifacts from our box? I pondered to myself. Ping! A light bulb came on in my mind, we needed to return to the crime scene to investigate. "Bring your phone and follow me," I commanded as I took off towards the basement without a shred of fear unworried about the Minotaur creature that could be lurking down there.

As we starting walking back towards the basement, I checked for anything that would be out of the ordinary. Yet the only thing noticeable was the layers of dust piling up like the sands of time had been spilled on the entire room. Nothing seemed too out of place until I saw some scuffled footprints off to the side of an aisle. I reached out my hand silently and Lina nodded. Creeping quietly around the corner we heard a voice whispering. I held up my hand, but it was too late. Lina kicked a box revealing our location.

Quickly glancing in the direction of pattering feet, I heard a creak, right before I was knocked to the floor. A whoosh of air sent dust swirling into a whirlwind as boxes burst open and spilled their contents all over the floor. Coughing I struggled to get up, but Lina's legs were trapping me. "Are you okay? I was worried we would get knocked out by that falling shelf. Sorry, I pushed you," Lina croaked.

"You're the one bleeding! I should be asking you if you are okay," I gasped, "Did someone push that on us intentionally?"

"I believe so. I am a tough bird and it would take more than some flimsy bookcase to do me in. Let's see if we can catch those jerks. I bet they are the same ones who took those artifacts from our box," replied Lina.

I scrambled to my feet and brushed off the clumps of debris whipping my head around to see which direction that they went in. Lina was pointing towards the door at the far side of the room. The red glow of the exit sign and the mysterious blinking letter x hung above the swinging door. We assumed that the trespassers must have fled in that direction. I hurried towards the door before it locked closed with Lina nipping at my heels.

Seeing a flash of black, I raced into the hallway only to notice that Lina was not behind me anymore. She seemed to be tugging on her shirt as the reddish thread was stuck in the door. Lina looked towards me and motioned for me to continue. Since she did not appear to be in any danger, I rounded the corner to look for the thieves.

Thump! I fell back stunned feeling as if I had run into a wall and looked up to see Alex standing before her with his arms crossed while tapping a foot. "Why aren't you doing your artifact inventory? Just because it's not as exciting as digging up a new artifact does not make it less important. Interns never get that!"

"Umm that's not it at all. Didn't you see those degenerates run by you? They stole our artifacts from the box. I tried telling the director, but she insists I just misplaced them. You have to help me catch them, and I am not falling for that minotaur act again!" I insisted.

"Well I didn't see anyone and I wouldn't call the minotaur an act if I were you. I wouldn't want to anger the beast," Alex said in a serious tone, "It's been a long day. Why don't you go home and rest?"

Starting to dislike his handsome white smile and laughing deep blue eyes, I narrowed my eyes to reply, "Are you really here to help? Or is your goal just to torture the interns? If that's the case, then you are succeeding."

Alex rubbed his hand over his brow and appeared to be remorseful as he spoke, "I suppose I am being a jerk, but I can't be too nice otherwise others will think I'm giving you special treatment. I'll stop torturing you as you called it, if you stop causing trouble. Deal?"

I frowned debating on if I believed him or not and started to say, "But I'm not causing trouble....."

Lina came up behind me and whispered, "Hey we should get out of here. It's about time to close."

Looking back at Alex, I decided not to argue and turned on my heel and stalked to the elevator. I exchanged a knowing glance with Lina as I hit the button for the top floor. I saw Alex's confused face as the doors whooshed closed. Leaning back against the back of the elevator I huffed out a breath of frustration as I squeezed my eyes shut.

Who knew that taking this internship would be so stressful? Minotaurs, pranks, stolen artifacts, and cranky directors were not quite what I had bargained for when I signed up to learn more about my past. Most people's journey into their family tree involved a computer, some old photos, and perhaps some records. Perhaps my summer was not going to be a vacation after all.

Opening my eyes, I looked over at Lina and said, "Hey, I'm going to my aunt's. I need to digest what all just happened today and come up with a game plan. Text me later?" She nodded and mentioned that she was late for a meeting.

As I left the museum, I noticed that it appeared to be more crowded outside and I saw several people carrying signs while walking down the street. Looking closer I saw that they were protesting the oil drilling. Not really wanting to get caught up in madness that might ensure, I skedaddled across the street.

The hair on the back of my neck stood up once I made it to the other side and scanned the crowd. I noticed a man in a grey trench coat, holding a pipe with his dark hat pulled down low over his eyes. He was halfway behind a lamp post and was staring straight at me following my every move. I wondered why I would be of interest to anyone who has to lurk in bushes. I pulled my brows together and brushed my chestnut hair out of the way. Feeling a bit nervous, I ducked into a coffee shop. From inside, I watched to see if the man would follow me.

I felt a hand on my shoulder and jerked in surprise. Peering up, I looked into deep chocolate eyes and had to blink back to reality when I heard, "Are you ok?" Without missing a beat, I replied, "I am now,", then flushed in embarrassment at my coy response. Noticing his badge, I quickly felt my face turn cherry red.

"Oh, I'm fine. Just getting used to city life and looking for my aunt. Thanks for checking on me though. I should get going," I quickly stammered before sneaking out the side door. With a quick glance I noticed that neither the police officer or the man was following me thank goodness.

I kept my hat low over my face, she would recognize me in a heartbeat! Silly fool! I should've stayed more out of sight. Apparently, being chased by an allegorical monster wasn't so scary after all. I should've added some blood or something for effect. I tossed the minotaur costume into the dumpster.

In spite of myself I couldn't help but feel a surge of pride at her fortitude, yet I pushed it down. Ugh! Don't go letting feelings get in the way. Once she finds out who I am she will never return those feelings anyways. Our romance if we were to have one was doomed from the time the stars aligned. She may as well be a Capulet and I a Montague.

Nope, no more being nice I steeled myself. I may as well cut her down now. Ruin her confidence and then hopefully she will go crying back to her mommy and daddy. The plan was almost in motion. T'would be a shame to have it go south.

From behind the thick pine bushes I had thought I was impossible to see. Yet, I saw her peer out of the coffee shop and look directly at me. Thankfully, I saw fear not recognition in her beautiful face. Making a quick decision I started to move towards her. My action got the desired result because she turned and ran!

Great I made her more scared, but I didn't want her to be scared of me. Or did I? Oh gosh darn this was confusing indeed! My advice is don't be an international artifact kleptomaniac in one of the oldest crime families in Russia and hope to to capture the heart of a future archaeologist.

She seems scared enough now to leave things be. I'd hate to have to step up the scare tactics. I dropped my fake cigarette to the ground and crushed the disguise with my blue sneaker. I whipped off the suspicious looking hat and coat and stuffed them into the bushes. Then followed her.

Chapter 8

Ring ring! Standing at my aunt's front door I rang the antique brass ringer, spinning it around a few times. The heavy oak door opened as my aunt said, "You can use your key, I won't get mad. So how are you settling in at the Smithsonian?"

"Uh, it's going okay. It's a little confusing and a little different than I had pictured it when I applied, but I am learning a lot," I hedged debating on how much I should tell her.

"I'm sure you will get the hang of it, dear. You are your mother's daughter. She always pushed her way through any problem," Aunt Margaret chuckled, "You do remind me of her."

"Really? I don't remember much about her and they don't really talk about her. Although, to be fair I don't really ask either. I'm sort of afraid to make them feel inadequate as parents if I want to know more about my birth mother and father," I mumbled.

"Oh dear, they would never think that. They probably don't want to stir up bad memories. Maybe we can have a girls' night, have some tea, and talk about her? Would you like that?" she inquired.

"That would be great!" I exclaimed.

My aunt smiled as she walked over to get her purse, "How about tomorrow? I have a meeting tonight that can't be rescheduled. Sorry, dear. Here is a takeout menu and I left some cash by the sink."

She slid out of the apartment door before I could say bye and was left wondering what I should do. Rather than sit around twiddling my thumbs, I went over and checked out the take-out menu. I saw a few things I wanted and used an online app to order some pork egg rolls and General Tso's chicken.

While waiting on the food delivery, I pulled out my tablet and started to research what was going on. I googled, "minotaurs in the Smithsonian" and saw nothing credible except a blog that talked about the hoax created by interns to scare the newbies. Feeling a little dumb, I decided to look more into the oil drilling protest. Even though I didn't want to be involved, I wanted to be more informed as to what was going on. Who knows, it might even have something to do with my missing artifacts. Doubtful, but might as well look into it.

After what seemed like only moments of researching on the bright screen I heard the buzzer indicating that someone wanted in the building. I saw the Chinese food take out logo and went down to meet the delivery guy. I paid the bill and brought it back up to the apartment to continue with my research. I saw a few articles pop up about how the pipeline was going through what some claimed was religious ground for the Navajo. This must have been what her cousin had been talking about.

Kai: [Hey are you free tonight? I just read an article about what's happening.]

Johana: [Tonight, I can't. But I can meet for lunch tomorrow. I can even meet you near the Smithsonian.]

Kai: [Great. I saw a coffee shop across the street. How does that sound?]

Johana: [Perfect. Gotta run.]

It seemed like everyone was busy with a purpose except me. After a moment I corrected myself because I had an active night of researching ahead of me. Clicking around led me from site to site. A headline caught my eye, but it was from another country, "Newly found artifacts change country border". After reading it for a few minutes, I got the gist of it. A group of people were able to prove they lived somewhere first by finding artifacts that had been lost to time.

Soon I noticed the screen starting to blur and my eyes fluttering shut. Before I knew I had slumped over on the velvety couch. I must have been pretty exhausted because I fell into a deep sleep fairly quickly.

I awoke to whispering voices. Blinking my eyes, I looked around the room and saw that I was surrounded my pots and several clay masks. Immediately, I thought, "Did my aunt go on a shopping trip?" Looking around the room, I realized that I was not in my aunt's house, but back in the artifact basement. Oh goodness I hoped I hadn't slept walked here. How embarrassing would that be? I glanced around and realized that I was perched up on one of the shelves. As I shook my head a golden-brown feather floated down. Pointing my head down I noticed that I was resting on sharp clawed feet that were gripping the top of a shelf.

As if my night could not get any weirder I began to hear the whispering voices more clearly and figured out it was the artifacts themselves talking. One in particular stood out, it was a rounded vase that was curved. Its sides were ornately decorated with a design with alternating colors of onyx and burnt clay. I also noticed a turquoise pendant lying beside the pot that was shaped like a falcon with a ruby for its eye. The whisper increased until I could hear the voice say, "Take care with yourself. The evil is coming."

I screeched, "What evil?" Then looked around to see who made that awful sound and looked embarrassed when I realized that sound came from myself.

"The evil is coming soon. Get out now. It's too late to save us, but only you can stop it now," the voice came from the pendant.

"Wait! How can you speak? What witchcraft is this?" I asked.

I heard a rumble then, "It's not witchcraft, but the voices of the ancients. We are your ancestors and we are here to help. But you have to find your own way." The voice faded into nothing and all was quiet.

The sounds of footsteps echoed throughout the basement and I saw light slashing through the air. The wobble of a flashlight indicated someone was running with it. I was torn between wanting to warn security and being concerned for my own safety. I tried sneaking towards the door only to remember that I was in fact a bird and while I could not sneak, I could fly. However, this presented a dilemma because what security guard would listen to a bird?

Quickly deciding not to call out an alarm, I saw an open half window and quickly tried to fly towards it. Still rather clumsy at the whole flying thing, I flapped this way and that. I felt my wing graze a shelf knocking me sideways. Then I felt the sting of light in my eyes as someone pointed the flashlight at me. "Hey what's a falcon doing in here? That's weird. Let's get out of here!" Even though I thought the intruders might leave, being caught in the light struck me with fear. Fighting down my panic, I concentrated really hard and tried to visualize myself flying. Ha! It worked! To my amazement I was flying and steered myself towards the open window and to freedom leaving the intrigue of the dark night in the basement.

What the heck was that? A hawk? How on Earth did one of those things get into the basement? I heard it's wings beating wildly as it frantically looked for a way out. Looking the crazed bird in the eye it seemed familiar somehow. Luckily for us it escaped out an open window without setting off an alarm.

My partner and I breathed an audible sigh of relief. Carefully, we wrapped up the artifacts we came to procure and arranged them in a duffle bag. One that anyone would normally take to the gym. Not wanting to take any chances of getting caught since the hawk sighting had been a close one we took only the two most valuable pieces. Scrambling I made sure my plastic mask to skew my face from cameras was still in place, I searched for the best route to avoid tripping any of the alarms that were laser beams across shooting across the hallways. With our backs to the wall we slinked through the hallways towards the emergency exit. I put in the pin number and the door beeped to open.

We were free and successful at that! I wiped the sweat from the back of my neck with my sleeve. Whew! Was I glad we got the first stop of our plan completed without a hitch. I handed off the bag to my accomplice, "Sell these on the black market or dark web. I don't care just make sure that the museum can never find them," I muttered in a hushed tone.

"Of course. That is what I do best," he replied giving me a toothy grin his Russian accent very thick, "I believe this concludes our business. Much luck to you."

I watched him blend in with the night hoping to never have to see him again. If there was no evidence that the land the artifacts came from was a grave or sacred land then NAGPRA (Native American Grave Protection Repatriation Act) would not apply. Then our pipeline could continue as planned, keeping us rich for generations to come. So what if we used substandard building materials and there would be leaks. I wondered sarcastically. We could just donate some drinking water and write it off our taxes. Or the locals could just move. Who would want to live in such an inhospitable place anyways?

"Kai! Kai!" I heard my name being shouted and someone shaking me awake. Frantically, I opened my eyes to see that it was my aunt and she was shaking my arm and not a wing. Phew! I was sort of worried that I was a falcon. Either I was having some strange dreams or I needed to talk to someone like yesterday about this.

I blinked a few times trying to wake up and my aunt's voice became clearer. "Kai, are you okay? You were shouting and flailing your arms around like a madwoman!" Aunt Margaret said sternly with her voice full of worry. She reached out a plucked a downy feather from my hair. "Were you ripping apart a pillow?"

Rubbing my eyes, I replied, "I'm fine. I must have been having a bad dream. Today at the museum one of the interns played a trick on me."

"What kind of trick?" inquired my aunt.

"Well someone switched our artifact box for an empty one making me think the artifacts were stolen. Before that an intern tried to convince me that there was a minotaur living in the basement. I feel sorta lame for falling for either trick," I mumbled as I hung my head.

Aunt Margaret reached out a well-manicured hand and put her index finger under my chin and lifted my face up. Once I met her eyes she said, "You are not lame. People in D.C. can be a bit different than in Boulder. Don't worry you will learn from their deception and not fall for it again. There is nothing to be ashamed of for wanting to see the best in people. But now is as good time as any to learn to that people aren't always who you expect them to be."

"Thanks! Maybe we could have that talk tomorrow night?" I ventured.

"You bet! I will clear my schedule. We both have to get up early though, so I'm going to call it a night," said my aunt as she gave me a kiss on the head.

I padded my way back to my bedroom and shook out some fawn colored feathers. At first, I was a bit hesitant about going back to sleep since I did not want go back to what was happening previously before my aunt came home. Yet once I crawled into bed and turned off the light it wasn't long until I felt myself fall into a restful sleep.

Chapter 9

The next morning, I woke up to the rich aromatic smell of coffee brewing. I breathed in the scent deeply, then threw off the covers and joined my aunt in the kitchen. I made myself a parfait with some fresh raspberries, granola, and vanilla yogurt and poured a cup of coffee. Pulling out a chair I sat beside my aunt who was looking through the paper and said, "Good morning." I murmured back sleepily.

I glimpsed the main story on the cover of the newspaper. The headline read, "Artifacts Go Missing from Smithsonian!" I was so surprised that I spat out the sip of water I just took. "Are you okay, dear?" my aunt asked. I nodded while coughing and pointed to the cover story. She flipped the paper over and gasped, "Oh my! What a terrible thing. I wonder what was stolen." We started reading through the paper and I saw the pictures of the turquoise falcon pendant and pottery and almost choked on my coffee. She said, "Oh this is not good at all. Any theft is a problem, but these artifacts are of special importance to the Navajo tribe. They are quite ancient and are linked with their legends of how they came to live in the area."

"Oh no! Will that affect anything? I heard that they might do oil drilling there," I wondered.

"I'm sure it could, but only time will tell. Hopefully, they catch the thief before they sell or damage the artifacts," My aunt tsked.

I swallowed my breakfast with my mouth suddenly feeling dry. Those were the same artifacts in my dream last night. Should I mention that I was witnessed this crime or just go about my business? I didn't want to invite too much scrutiny as I wasn't sure if she would believe me or just commit me to an asylum. Cautiously testing the waters, I decided to dip my toes in the water metaphorically speaking. "I had a dream about those exact same artifacts, but I had never seen them before," I started.

My aunt looked at me quickly with surprise and said, "Oh? What do you suppose that means?"

"I don't know. I was hoping you could tell me?" I inquired nervously.

"Well it's not me inside your head, so there are some things that only you can answer," she responded.

I wasn't sure if I liked that answer and needed to do some thinking. Maybe Lina might have some answers if I should even tell her. I finished my breakfast and told my aunt that I would think about it. As I was walking I noticed a hawk soaring high above me, circling as if waiting for me. Then it glided off and landed on a tree along the sidewalk ahead.

I heard, "Hey Kai!" I turned around and saw a classmate. I forgot her name at the moment, but she was funny. I waved and asked her how her first days were going. "Oh just swell, doing all the running around. I'm sort of jealous, I heard you got to go on an artifact hunt. I just get to run after coffee. Oh did you see the head of interns? Alex. Wheweee. Those eyes could melt a heart. Anyways gotta run. Maybe I can surpass you," she said with a laugh and sped across the street.

I was still wondering what she meant when I heard Lina say, "Hey you alright. You look like you saw a ghost."

"Where did you come from? Sneaking up on people isn't very nice," I shot her a perturbed glance. Then felt bad for being grouchy towards her, she had just tried to help me. "Sorry, I didn't mean to snap at you."

"It's okay. Seriously though, you can talk to me if you need to. I do prefer that to grouchiness. Are you mad because Alex has a lot of admirers?" Lina said while angling her head towards Alex being swarmed by a gaggle of girls.

Shaking my head, I said, "Do you know anything about dreams?"

"That sounds vague, ominous, and deep. I have dreams, if that's what you mean. Did you dream something strange?" Lina asked while falling in step with me as we walked towards the lecture hall.
"We're going to be late, we should get inside," I hastened.

Once we made it into the auditorium everyone had a seat and got out their notebooks ready to learn. There were at least one hundred people all of whom went silent once the director walked up on the stage. Her coiffed ash blonde hair was neat at the base of her neck and her grey pant suit both blended into the background and stood out. She walked confidently to the stage and there was a slight quiver to her voice that gave away she was not as calm as she appeared to be. "Attention everyone, if you have not seen the news then this will be the first time you hear about this. There was a theft last night at the museum. We don't have information at this time on the criminals, but we are looking through our security tapes. Two major items were taken related from the Navajo collection. These artifacts had been on display but were in cleaning in the basement during the time of the robbery. Since the artifact lab is now a crime scene we have assigned several interns to go to the Navajo reservation to do their artifact collection, sorting, and more there. That is all the information I have at the moment. Check the halls for your reassignment," announced the director.

"I saw that last night!" I leaned over and whispered to Lina.

She turned her head sharply, "You saw what?"

"Shhh" I put a finger to my lips, "I don't want the whole auditorium to hear you! I'm still not quite sure if it was a dream or if I actually saw it."

"You need to tell me everything!" Lina whispered urgently.

I nodded, then looked back towards the stage to see the director walking down the stairs. I saw Alex walking towards the mic as he went over what to do once you figured out your assignment. He also stated that we would not be allowed in the basement today at all and it was preferred that we stay on this floor.

We got up and followed the others into the hallway. While we were trying to be orderly, there was some shoulder bumping and crushed toes as the crowd of people tried to see the different lists in the hall. "You would think that they would have just emailed us the lists or something? That would have been less chaotic," I whispered to Lina while taking a strange elbow to the back.

Eventually, I found my name on a list. I was to go to a dig site on the Navajo reservation. I looked over the list and did not see Lina's name. She just shrugged and said, "I will talk to my father." I felt my phone vibrate in my leather bag and pulled it out. I had a text from my cousin letting me know she was free to meet shortly.

"Hey I'm going to meet my cousin for coffee. Can we meet up this afternoon before we go to separate places?" I asked Lina.

"I will see, if not then I will see you at the dig site," she replied.

I found it a bit odd that she was so sure that she would go. She didn't even look at the other lists. Well either I would see her later or not, no sense in worrying about it too much. I checked the list again after she slipped away in the crowd and didn't see her name anywhere. There must be a mistake. However, I did notice that Alex was going with my group.

Chapter 10

My cousin saw me come in and waved me over to her table. She had already gotten me an iced hibiscus tea and was sipping something with extra shots of espresso in it. No wonder she had so much energy! Johanna had a briefcase full of notes and writing pads that she was going through as I sat down. "Hey cousin long time, no see," I said as I gave her a smile, "You look like you have been busy." I pointed to her stack of notes.

She smiled back and replied, "Well it's a big job fighting corporations. Turns out that I don't have enough information for a case at this time. I might have to go back to the reservation to gather more evidence and get others to come with me to Washington."

"What exactly are you trying to do? I'm a little confused, but my parents try to keep us away from politics. Something about us being too young and such," I explained.

Johanna raised an eyebrow, "Well it could be because both of your parents were activists and they want to keep you out of trouble. Myself, I sort of like danger and taking down bad guys using the law seems like a good way to channel the energy."

"Who are the bad guys and what are they trying to do?" I asked, "I saw something about the pipeline, but other than that I am sort of clueless."

"While not all companies are bad in this case, the bad guys are a pipeline trying to go through our sacred ground and right through a major drinking water source. This same company has had several pipeline breaks which have leaked oil into the surrounding area," grumbled Johanna.

"Why can't they just put the pipeline somewhere else? Especially if it's causing so many problems. There is a ton of empty space out west. It seems silly to fight over strips of it," I interjected.

Johanna shrugged and replied, "That would make sense wouldn't it? The elders even offered some land to the south of the village to be used for the pipeline. It wouldn't interfere with the water nor with sacred land. However, the company claims that rerouting the pipeline would cost millions of dollars in plans and extra pipeline."

"Sounds like you are in a hard place. Actually, I am going out to the reservation tomorrow with my studies. Perhaps I can see this all firsthand!" I jauntily replied.

Smiling she promised, "I will have to come out and show you the area. There is so much of your history there, plus you can get a chance to meet Ahiga, our grandfather. He was a code talker. Did you know that?"

"What? No way! I can't believe I didn't know what a cool life he had!" I blurted.
"Yes, his legacy is what drives me to do better. I'm surprised you didn't know. I wish I would have gotten in contact with you when you were younger, but I did not want to interfere with your adopted parents. They seemed rather fearful and worried that you would choose not to live with them," Johanna carefully explained.

I pondered everything Johanna had just said. I was curious if my adoptive parents who were really my dad's brother and his wife if they had meant to keep me from learning about my past. They had always loved me and treated me like a daughter. They even encouraged me to apply at the Smithsonian, so I refused to think that they intended to rob me of fulling knowing myself and my past. Yet, it was hard not to be mad at them. I could have had spent more time with this grandfather learning his stories, but now I had less time with him.

Shaking it off, I looked up into Johanna's onyx eyes and said, "Thank-you. I can't wait to learn more. When are you going out there?"

"I need to finish up a few things here, but I will be out by the end of the week," she added while typing up an email, "Actually, I should probably be getting back to the office. I want to catch several congressmen before they go on vacation."

I mumbled, "See you later," and picked up my tea to leave the coffee shop more confused than when I had entered. I should've asked her about my dream, but I had forgotten. Perhaps I could ask her about it later on in the week or Lina. Maybe dreams were something else about my heritage that I didn't know about. Pulling out my smartphone I decided to look up some information while sitting on a bench. My aunt wouldn't be home for a few more hours and I had plenty of time to pack.

Several people were walking their dogs in the park weaving along the path guarded by large ancient oak trees. I noticed one dog sniffing its way towards me and it came over to sit beside me. Grinning I leaned down to give the golden retriever a pat on the head. It had a collar, but it's owner did not seem to be anywhere in sight. I giggled as it licked my fingers. The golden-brown eyes met mine and I made my decision. Something in those eyes made me feel at peace with telling my aunt what I had seen. I wasn't even that afraid anymore, well I was a bit, but I definitely not a run and hide kind of scared.

I gave the dog a last pat and got up to return to my aunts to pack when it wagged its tail and bounded back to its owner who was whistling for him. With steady feet, I walked through the rest of the park barely noticing the cherry trees blooming. I knew I needed help and I trusted my aunt to get me through.

I had just finished packing my suitcase when I heard the click of my aunt's heels as she entered the apartment. I dashed out to meet her and she looked surprised, "What are you doing home so early? Are you feeling okay?"

"Oh yea. They sent us home early due to the museum being a crime scene and I am being sent to the Navajo reservation," I replied casually.

"What?" gasped my aunt.

"Oh never mind that. I was really hoping we could have that talk now especially since I will be going to where my mom was raised," I suggested.

My aunt's deep blue eyes looked concerned with a storm cloud of emotion swirling in them and I could see the moment she relented and replied, "Alright. What do you want to know?"

"For starters how do I remind you of her? They never did say how she died either," I babbled quickly and started to ask more questions, then stopped myself so I could get the answers to the questions I already sought.

Running her hands through her thick salt and pepper curls she began, "Your mother was very brave and of course beautiful. She was studying law when she met your father who was studying archaeology. Together they moved to the reservation to fight for rights. Your mother always looked at every angle to a problem and pushed through it until it was solved. She won a case to guarantee clean drinking water and got grants to have several wells dug that are still in operation today. She just never gave up and I see that fighting spirit in you as well."

"Was she different?" I wondered quietly.

My aunt pursed her full ruby lips and stated, "Of course she was different. No one normal could capture your father's attention. You don't want to be normal, do you?"

"Well I mean did she ever have any special abilities? This sounds silly, but last night I dreamed out those artifacts and saw them get stolen. It was so realistic like I was there!" I burst out with a sharp cry. Then put a hand over my mouth worried that I had said too much.

My aunt's face softened as she looked at me with dismay and she softly patted my hand and asked, "What's been troubling you? I'm afraid I don't know much about any abilities, but I do know some Navajo myths and legends if that would help?"

"I haven't really felt like myself since I got that letter, I keep having dreams where I am flying. Not like in an airplane, but like I am a bird. It's confusing, but also feels natural. I don't know how to explain it. I feel a little ridiculous!" I hurried in exasperation.

My aunt sighed, stood up, and strode over to her grandiose ebony bookcase and looked thoughtfully at the middle section. With a look of triumph, she plucked a voluminous text from the shelf. Holding the ancient looking text that was timeworn and tattered around the edges she came back over next to me on the deep red couch. "This has the answers that you seek. Unfortunately, I cannot just tell you as speaking out loud about this topic is not allowed by superstition," Aunt Margaret explained calmly.

"What can't you talk about? Is there something wrong with me?" I implored.

She just shook her head and stated, "I can't talk about it. But I do know that you are a wonderful niece, smart, and kind. You will do harm to none that I can say." She smiled encouragingly and laid the heavy edition in my lap. "When do you leave?"

"I leave in the morning," I mumbled sadly as I ran my hands over the thick worn book. That's when I saw the title *Skin walkers* and I regarded the book with apprehension. I knew if I read more that my life would never be the same again. I tried to hand it back to her, but she pushed it more firmly into my hands and told me that it would make for great reading material for the plane ride. With that she left me sitting alone in the living room wondering what I should do.

Chapter 11

"Ladies and Gentlemen, this is your captain speaking. We are first in line for takeoff and we will land in Albuquerque, New Mexico at 9:30 local time. The weather is a chilly 92 degrees in the shade with a light breeze and mostly sunny. Make sure to fasten your seatbelts yet make yourself comfortable for the 4-hour flight," the pilot announced as we started to push off from the gate.

I nervously ran my fingers over the cover of the book my aunt had given me. It was here, I was here. I was surrounded by people and was about to be thousands of feet in the air. It seemed like there was no escaping it. It's not like it could hurt me and no one would notice.

Using both hands I carefully opened the text letting a whoosh of ancient dust out. I secretly hoped that it wasn't poison. Who knew what was hidden inside? I had seen enough movies to know how opening an old book could end. My face could melt off, I could contract smallpox or the plague, or be given second sight.

Thankfully, none of those things occurred at least not yet. I peeked my eyes over the large volume to make sure no one was watching me too carefully since I could not shake the feeling that I was under surveillance. Looking down at the first page I saw a beastly picture of a man turning into a wolf and the word, Yenaldooshi, written under the picture. I couldn't be a werewolf, could I? Feeling the hairs on my arm stand up I kept reading and realized that there was a legend of the Yenaldooshi which was a shapeshifter of sorts. These shapeshifters weren't always wolves but could be birds as well.

Intrigued I read on. Only to find out that these skin walkers were often said to be cursed because of a sin they had committed and were seeking to harm others. This type of shapeshifter had to actually put on the skin of the animal that they wished to transform into. However, I never recalled ever doing this and it always occurred during a dream. I hoped that I hadn't committed something horrible while I was sleeping. Perhaps, I was different. I mean I didn't feel evil, evil things feel evil right? I decided to keep reading only to doze off in the middle of how skin walkers begin their transformation.

I awoke to a hand on my shoulder, "Miss, miss. The plane has landed. It's time to deplane," a nice, but firm flight attendant told me. I jerked my head around and thankfully there were no werewolves in sight. Gathering up my belongings and stuffing them into my oversized handsewn leather purse that my brother had made for me, I made my way off the plane. Weaving through the airport I made my way to the baggage claim. I dragged my luggage off the carousel and headed over towards a man holding a sign, "Smithsonian interns" and waited patiently. Within the hour several more people from my class showed up, but no Lina.

Alex's well combed blonde head bobbed through the crowd heading towards us. I was surprised and asked, "They sent you this way?"

"Who else will keep you all on the straight and narrow?" he responded with a devastating wink intended to make the girls around swoon I presumed.

Several of the girls giggled while the lone boy of the group groaned in annoyance. I tried not to blush, but I couldn't help it. While it was difficult to resist his charms, I felt that I must. I retorted saucily, "Maybe it is us who has to keep you on the straight and narrow."

"Oh Miss Kai! You don't know how right you are," he tossed back. His grin indicated that he could turn any barb that I threw at him into honey. I resisted saying anything back. "I do have an uncle working in the area and he did try to pull a few strings to get me come out this way. There are a few reasons why I decided to go hang out in the desert versus my nice air-conditioned office," Alex offered coolly.

My mind went on instant alert, he had family here too? He didn't look Navajo, I wonder what his uncle was doing here. Maybe we had more in common than I initially thought. I peeked over at him from under my thick dark lashes and saw that he caught my stare and held it back until my cheeks turned red.

"Ahem. I don't mean to interrupt, but the van is going to leave without you. It's a long dry walk through the desert to our village of Tohatchi," smirked a tall young man with a deep rich voice.

Embarrassed I looked over at him and saw that he was very handsome with his long jet-black hair pulled back with a tong at the nape of his neck. He flashed me a white toothy grin that for some reason reminded me of a pirate. It may have been the way that he smiled a little crooked with one side of his mouth curled up knavishly like he was up to no good. Meeting his obsidian eyes, I felt something that I hadn't felt before and vaguely seemed as if I had been sucker punched. I saw recognition flash on his face as he spun around and waved everyone to follow him. I overheard some of the girls' giggle about how they wouldn't mind being trapped in the desert with such handsome guys.

"Guess we are stuck with a bunch of star struck girls for this venture," whispered one of my classmates to me. "Hi, I'm Emily. I don't remember running into you during orientation, but you look sensible enough. Perhaps we can be lab partners?"

"Uh maybe. Don't they pick them for us?" I fumbled for an answer. I wasn't really sure I wanted to be her partner and was hoping Lina was going to make it.

"Probably, but if we tell them we were already paired up at the Smithsonian then they will let us work together," Emily answered coyly.

I wrinkled my brow, "Wouldn't that be lying?" I was always an honest person and even a white lie didn't sit well with me.

Emily blinked, "Well I guess you are right. Sorry, it seems I managed to get off on the wrong foot with my only ally."

"It's okay," I mumbled. Emily kept chattering on about how she first got interested in archaeology and the Navajo. I felt bad, but I just sort of tuned her out. She seemed to enjoy going on about things.

Chapter 12

The ride started out smooth since it was all highway and noisy as we had the windows down to keep the temperature reasonable in the van. Apparently, we weren't going riding the whole way with the luxury of air conditioning. If he worn 80s seat covers were any indication we would be lucky if the van made it down the highway due to its age. The mysterious driver had the radio up pretty loudly blaring some old rock and roll. Lucky for me, I enjoyed some Led Zepplin even though judging by some of the other's faces they weren't happy with the music selection. Once we passed all the skyscrapers of Albuquerque the landscape quickly transformed into what seemed like a barren wasteland of dry sand and rocks. Yet, I began so see colors emerge from the rocks indicating that the desert was much more complex than at first glance. Rust and sienna colored layers painted jagged rock faces making them appear to be monochromatic lasagna showing off different millennia of Earth's past. I pointed it out the layers to Alex who smiled approvingly of my knowledge of stratigraphy.

We turned off the highway onto a smaller road that had seen it's better days, but still seemed to be paved. On this road we couldn't go quite as fast so you could see various cacti from the van, some were pipe shaped, and juniper bushes dotted the flat horizon along with a few spruce trees in the distance. A little more green was mixed in with the shades of brown adding to the painter's palate. The early afternoon sun was bright and the road had a bit of a glare coming off the white paint. My eyes met the driver's sunglass obscured eyes in the rearview mirror and I wondered how long he had been watching me watch the surrounding area.

Bump! Ouch! Several of the girls screamed out when we hit a bump and the driver said, "Sorry ladies and gentleman. We have entered the Navajo Nation where the federal government doesn't pave the roads." He angled his head towards the roads and the piles of pavement on either side of the road. "We make do with a simpler existence here. Therefore, the bumpy roads will continue until we reach the village. If you feel like you are going to fall out of your seat, please grab ahold of the bars on the ceiling. We are going on an off-road adventure. If you see a cliff be kind enough to warn me, we wouldn't want the mountain lions feasting on us tonight," his husky voice continued with a touch of amusement.

A few gasps were heard as we continued to bump along with the van occasionally swerving left or right to avoid colossal pot holes. I was slightly worried that our luggage which was perched atop the van would fall off at any time. We rode in silence for what seemed hours before we hit a particularly large pothole. I bounced up and hit the ceiling, then landed with a hard oomph back in my seat. Perhaps this was why we were normally supposed to wear a seatbelt. Even though the back seat did not have any.

I noticed that we had stopped moving and asked Emily, "Do you know why we have stopped?"
She replied, "I think perhaps a tire has blown out. Maybe he will get out and take a look. Hopefully, there is a spare somewhere." with an indignant tone.

Just then the driver opened the door and walked around the side of the white, but rusty van. Then he popped his head in the side door and called, "Looks like a flat. Everyone needs to get out so we can jack the van up. Anyone know how to change a tire?"

We all filed out of the van one by one and stood by the edge of the gravel road. Several were trying to fight over the shade created by the van and others were slinking off to the juniper bushes to sit down under their slim shade. I watched as the driver pulled a jack from under the front seat and a tire iron. His strong dark hands pulled out a tool box, then he set those beside the tire. Opening the tool box, he set about prying the spare tire from the back of the van. Rolling it over to the flat busted tire, he held up the tire iron and asked, "Does anyone know where this goes?" Alex and several girls looked at each other then back at him with a look of fear and Alex mouthed something about being doomed.

With a deep chuckle he wiped his hands on his dark jeans and got down to get to work. I saw that he needed some help after he placed the jack and went over to hold the lug nuts as he took them off the tire. His dark eyes met mine and I almost dropped what he handed me. Trying to make the situation a little less awkward I started a conversation, "So did you grow up here? Or are you just working at the dig site too?"

With a laugh he tossed his head back and muscled through taking off the last lug nut, "I grew up here. I wouldn't say I am working on the site per say. I have my misgivings about even digging up our past and putting it on display. No one wants their grandfather's remains and possessions to be in a museum. Yet, since this is what the tribe wants I can see the benefits. Why are you here? You want a summer adventure?" His tone becoming slightly sarcastic and almost insulting.

Prickling a little bit, I snapped, "Well one would assume I am here to study the Navajo artifacts. No reason to insult me thinking I just wanted a little fun. I have spent years studying to get into the intern program. It's not something I did on a whim. You'll find that I'm a hard worker and take my work seriously." Holding onto my turquoise necklace, I saw him glance down questionably. Then I dropped the lug nuts and sulked over to chat with the girls. If he thought I just wanted to gossip and be helpless, then I sure wasn't going to help him.

Out of the corner of my eye I saw him shake his head, mutter under his breath, and keep working. Alex sauntered over to him and said, "I can suppose I can give you a hand unless you care to insult me as well?"

"I've got it. Don't trouble yourself. Your hands look like they've been in a museum and not up for this sort of work anyways," he replied snidely.

"What a lovely chauffeur we have," Alex grumbled, "We shall just wait over here in the hot sun and slowly melt while we wait for you to muscle through it alone."

I felt bad for our driver even if he had insulted me. Seeing how the rest of the crew were acting I could see why he might have a low opinion of people coming to the dig. Alex could be quite a jerk to others, which was at odds with how nice he could be to me at times.

Feeling the sweat trickle down the back of my neck I was beginning to wonder how much longer we were going to be stranded out here. Checking my phone, I saw that I had no cell service, so there was no texting anyone or getting help if the tire didn't get changed. Peering up I saw that I was alone by the road, I twirled and saw no one in sight, but the van. Then a hand hit the glass of the window causing me to jump. It was Emily trying to wave me over. While I had been distracted the bucket of rust had been fixed and we were ready to be on our way again if I decided to get back in the van that is. Feeling a little mortified, I hurried up and joined the crew inside.

Chapter 12

Upon reaching our destination I admit I was a little underwhelmed. Most of the village was a few concrete houses built near one another, a small community building that seemed to serve as a school and town hall, and several dusty cars. For some reason I had always envisioned the reservation filled with colors, artisans, traditional houses, and horses. Apparently, I had looked at my birthplace through rose colored glasses my whole life. It looked just a tad depressing. I wondered if Lina lived in one of these houses.

Seeing my look of disappointment, the driver said, "Don't worry. This is just where we take the tourists. I would caution you not to drink the water though, we are still fighting for clean drinking water."

As we got out of the dilapidated vehicle an older gentleman was waiting for us clipboard in hand. He did a double take on my necklace just like the driver did and wondered if he knew my mother since the pendant belonged to her. He introduced himself, "Welcome to Navajo Nation. I am Yas and this is Atsa," he announced and pointed towards the van driver, "We run the dig site alongside with the Smithsonian to ensure our history is handled properly. We will be taking you out to the site tomorrow. Today, you will go on a tour of a few villages as well as partake in a welcome dinner to introduce you to people with whom you will be working." He kept talking while I glanced around hoping to see if my cousin had already made it here or if Lina was around. Despite my best efforts, I failed to spot either one. Which wasn't that difficult to determine as there were not many others here. "This is just the outpost of the community where we have guests check in who are entering the territory. Go ahead and get back in the van and we will go to your lodgings first so you can unpack your belongings."

Spying her standing in the scorching desert sun talking to a village elder, I thought this was an interesting turn of events. Who knew she'd be sent here too. I should let the others know that we might have a problem, and she could foil our plans.

What if she recognized us? I was beginning to fear that she suspected something. She knew more about the museum heist than she let on. I still wasn't sure what she knew or how she knew. The only certainty was that she undeniably had acted differently afterwards. I could tell she wasn't herself. Maybe my fears were unfounded, but if she kept sticking her nose where it didn't belong, then I'd be forced to do something rash.

I had tried undermining her confidence, but clearly that didn't work. Perhaps a bit more of a severe scare was in order. I thought for a moment, then a plan brought a smile to lips. Yes, yes that ought to send her packing. Better scared than dead I always figured. Death was on the table if she interfered with our purpose.

Inwardly groaning about having to get back into the scorching van with it's warm musty purple seats, I tried to sneak in towards the front this time so I could get out quickly. The heat was getting to me as living in Boulder, it did not get hot frequently. Sensing my discomfort Yas rolled down his window to let in some fresh air. I smiled over at him warmly. I thought about asking about my grandfather but was a little unsure. Yas looked away quickly, but before he did I thought I saw a look of fear and anger on his face. I wasn't sure what I had done already, but perhaps I could change my mind.

Ping! My phone alerted me to an endless stream of texts. I must have gotten back into a cell service area. Seeing a text from my parents, I replied to ease their worry letting them know that I was on the reservation safely. Then I saw a text from my cousin.

Johana: [Looks like I will be on a flight out tomorrow. I just told Atsa to help you out and make you feel welcome. He's my fiancé's little brother. I will introduce you to our grandfather when I get out there.]

Kai: [Not Atsa! I already started off on the wrong foot with him.]

Johanna: [I'm sure he will get over it. He's been looking forward to meeting you since I showed him your Facebook profile in early spring. Something about wanting to help you rediscover your heritage.]

I made a face at my phone. I'd really stuck my foot in it this time, but to be fair Atsa wasn't exactly being welcoming. Regarding him thoughtfully, I saw that he was being very patient with Yas and was helping give him directions. It may be that I was wrong about him, but I suppose I would soon find out.

Alex's voice interrupted my thoughts, "I'm glad we didn't get stuck in the desert. It seems like a dreadful place to be abandoned. It might be a little dangerous being out here with no phone service and on a dig site that is haunted by the past."

"Haunted? What do you mean haunted?" I inquired with interest.

Alex nervously looked around the van, "Well it is a graveyard. I'm sure someone put a curse on it and I heard on all who enter."

"I thought you were an archaeologist not a myth chaser, Alex. You sound as if you are scared of doing your job and from what I hear terribly misrepresenting the Navajo people," I chastised.

"Curse? Did I hear curse? You all were cursed the moment you set foot on the blood-stained sand," Atsa said with a wry grin indicating he was joking.

The van full of people all laughed for a moment as we pulled up to our lodgings. While I had expected a building of some sort, I realized that I saw none. There were only a group of tents pitched together around a fire pit and a larger open tent that vaguely resembled a tepee. A shocked voice cried out, "Is that where we are staying? It does not look like there is even running water or electric? However will I wash my hair or style it?" We all heard the dismay in her voice.

While another voice, "Great this is what I am talking about. This is true archaeology. Going and being one with what we are studying, away from all the modern conveniences. This is truly how archaeology is supposed to be."

I figured I was somewhere in the middle as I wasn't worried about my hair, yet I did not feel some sort of deeper connection just because we didn't have electricity. That sounded a bit hipsterish for me. Yet, seeing as how the comment came from a young man wearing Indiana Jones get up, I could see he perhaps was a bit overzealous. It's not like we were discovering the Temple of Doom or rescuing people from an evil villain bent on taking over the world. Determined to look after myself and not seem too helpless or mortified about living a few weeks without electricity, I climbed out of the van and schlepped my stuff over to a tent with my student number on the front. It looked like I was sharing the text with another girl. She was quiet wearing her pale hair pulled back, a floppy hat, and glasses. Even though she seemed a bit standoffish at first, I was glad that I wasn't rooming with the girl who had shrieked. I never would get any sleep with her incessant talking and whining about how this wasn't like her summer cabin on Lake Michigan. The other girl smiled shyly and introduced herself, "Hi, I'm Amy,"

I held out a hand and replied, "Kai, nice to meet you. I'm from Colorado. Where are you from?"

"California. Well northern California. I think we are going to be late for dinner, we best head up to the main tent," she quietly reminded me.

Chapter 13

Once we made it to the tent, wonderful smells wafted through the air. Everything was laid out in baskets with a stack of chipped plastic plates in the corner. Steam rose from the roasted corn which was glistening with yellow butter smelling sweet. A bowl of tricolor beans was beside what looked to be fry bread, also known as Indian bread. The large baked pieces of dough resembled pizza dough awaiting toppings. A savory smelling dish was filled high with chopped fire roasted meat pieces. Continuing on my way I saw a dish of what looked to be flowers. "How nice there are some flowers set out for us!" Amy exclaimed with the most excitement I had seen bubble out of her all day.

Stifling a laugh, Atsa appeared behind us seemingly from out of nowhere and stated, "Those are squash blossoms filled with blue corn mash. They are quite delicious. We decided to only slowly introduce you to some local food and saved the antelope liver for another time."

While my face turned green, I noticed that Amy seemed intrigued by the idea. She must be up for trying different foods or perhaps she liked liver. I saw him look over at Amy with a hint of admiration, and I felt a tingle of jealousy. Quickly, I pushed the thought away since I wasn't ready to look deeper into my feelings. Seeing Atsa walking towards the center of the pavilion, I noticed he picked up a microphone. "Excuse me everyone! First off welcome and I can't wait for us to enjoy some delicious food together. We wanted you to try some of our local dishes and my wife and daughters have been toiling all day to prepare this feast for you," Yas motioned to his family who was seated in a corner. A chorus of thank-yous erupted from the tent. Yas continued on, "We hope that this food brings you peace and happiness during your time here. I would tell a story about how we all came to be here, but I see a sea of hungry faces so at least I will say dig in!"

I had no memories of any of the food that my mother may have made for me and my adoptive parents had never tried fixing any Navajo dishes. With anticipation I filed into line anxious to try the food that my mother had grown up on. The delicious mix of smells made my stomach growl. Eventually, after what seemed hours, but I'm sure was minutes, I was able to pile a piece of fry bread with beans, corn, and roasted juicy meat. Out of curiosity I put several of the squash flowers on my dish.

Making my way towards a table with my group number on it, I choose a seat that was empty and started sampling the delights before me. Biting into the squash flower, I was surprised by the soft texture and sweet and savory taste of the filling. For some reason I had thought it would be tough. Spotting Indy across the table, that was my nickname for the guy who thought he was the next Indiana Jones. Thankfully, he wasn't carrying a whip with him glad that someone had told him that wasn't necessary for dinner. He was spinning a yarn about his previous field school experience, "That's when I got bit by a bot fly, then I whipped out my trusty swiss army knife and dug out all the eggs it laid before they could spread throughout my body. The doctor's still say I missed one and I will never know when it will crawl out of my ear and into the next victim! Right afterwards, I made the biggest find to come out of the Mayan ruins to date! The jade jaguar was just sitting there buried under some tree root."

"What was the purpose of the jade artifact? Did you write up an article for a magazine on your find?" Amy inquired in an innocent tone.

"Pshh I don't know. That's for some dork in a lab somewhere," Indy smirked confidently with a smug grin.

Amy whispered so only I could hear, "The idiot doesn't even know what he found if he even found it. Just a wanna be treasure hunter and not a true researcher of history."

"Why have artifacts in a museum if we don't know their purpose?" the field school director questioned with an inquisitive tone as he wandered by the table.

That seemed to deflate Indy's bragging for the moment. Instead he buried his face in his plate with his ears burning red. I almost felt sad for him. What a terrible way to start off with the director and to be put in your place too! Perhaps flying under the radar was a better way to start. A few others at the table tried to hide their laughter and I feared that many thought Indy was a bit boastful and a bit egocentric. Glancing around I failed to notice Alex anywhere about but did notice Atsa sitting over by Yas laughing at a joke.

I looked away hoping he didn't notice me watching him. Despite my attempt to be sly, Amy noticed where my gaze had lingered and grinned at me. She made a motion with her hand turning a key at her mouth showing that my secret was safe with her. Sharing a secret reminded me of my sister which made me miss home with a sharp pang. Yet, I made sure to smile back instead of revealing my homesickness.

After several hours of jokes, stories, and laughter I had forgotten my nostalgia for home and was enjoying the company of my comrades. Many of my fellow interns were from all over America and not quite as eccentric as Indy nor as whiny as some I had heard on the bus. Already, I was looking forward to working with them over the next few weeks at the dig site. What adventures were to be had. Several of them had been on several digs before and were anxious to share some tips with me. The best advice was to get lots of sleep because the sun seems to rise earlier in the desert and working all day in the sand could quite wear you out.

Yawning we said our good nights and I stumbled back through the camp with Amy with only one flashlight between us. "I hope there aren't any scorpions in this area. Just in case though, make sure to leave your boots on all the time and shake them out when you go to put them on in the morning," Amy mentioned casually. I stopped walking, scorpions? Why didn't I think about those creepy creatures before now? I had sort of wished she would not have mentioned that until the morning since now I would not sleep a wink in fear of scorpion crawling into my ear. I searched the ground as we walked, then once we arrived at our tent I waited for Amy to unzip the door. I peeked my head in and shone my flashlight around the floor of the tent, but no scorpions came flying at my face.

Carefully, I stepped into the tent after removing my boots and crawled over to my sleeping bag to pull back the one side. Looking down I screamed and fell backwards trying to claw my way out of the tent. "Oh gosh, Kai. I forgot to tell you the scorpions here aren't deadly. It's okay I can put it outside," Amy spoke softly and calmly.

"Noooo, it's not-t-t a-a scorpion!" I stammered. Amy pushed past me and looked in my sleeping bag and gasped. "Don't touch it!" I shouted with panic lacing my voice. I grabbed her arm from behind as we both stared down at the mutilated doll missing a leg and the button eye popped off. There was a sharp metal object protruding from the doll's chest with "Stop nosing around or this will be you!" scrawled across a torn piece of paper. The words seemed to drip blood making the scene all the more macabre.

The sounds of my scream must have drawn other's attention as everyone in the camp ran towards our tent to see what was going on. The director, Yas, and Atsa pushed their way to the front of the group. Yas demanded, "What is going on here?"

"Did someone get hurt? Or did the skin walker and scorpion stories just get to you guys?" the director asked with a mix of worry and humor.

Amy handed them the doll with the note attached. The men grew serious and they told everyone else, "Go back to your tents now!" I could tell by the look on their faces that no one wanted to do that, but they waivered under Yas' fierce scowl.

As some were leaving I heard someone whisper, "Guess it's true. This place really is haunted. I heard a couple went missing years ago. Maybe it's happening again!"

My ears perked up. A couple had gone missing years ago? I wonder if there was a connection with my parents? I filed that tidbit of information away to ask Lina when she got here tomorrow. A cough interrupted my thoughts and I saw Atsa inspecting my face with concern. "Sorry, what's happening?"

"The director asked if you had any enemies. If you had a fight with any of the other girls? He seems to think it's a prank of some sort," Atsa explained, "But Yas is concerned that since you are the granddaughter of Ahiga that you are in greater danger."

"I haven't even met him! Why would that put me in danger?" I demanded angrily while confusion spread over my face.

"That is for him to tell you," Yas murmured, "It is not up to me to disclose a man's secrets. I will take you to him tomorrow. He is unwell and can't travel. He will have been surprised and pleased to see his..."

"How do you know who my grandfather is?" I interrupted.

Yas looked at me patiently, "We know everything about you, Kai. Even the things you have yet to discover yourself."

"Hey what is going on here? I think we are going way beyond looking into a mean girl's joke on poor Kai here," interjected the director, "We don't need any more trouble this summer."

"There won't be any more trouble, I promise you!" I blurted, "Well it's been a long day, I'm exhausted." I elbowed my way into the tent and got in my sleeping bag. I squeezed my eyes shut and willed it all to go away.

Watching from the corner of camp, I saw that all of the commotion was over for now. The doll didn't quite frighten her enough into leaving. I was given a timeline and now I had less than a week to get her out of here or it would be out of my hands. I suppose I had to be more extreme next time.

Perhaps if I just talked to her, she would listen and stay out of this nasty business? Nah, that wouldn't work at all. She would probably just turn me in, which would put even more people in danger. Maybe I need to knock her out, give her food poisoning? Wait I have the best idea! What if I frame her? I could keep her out of it and also throw suspicion off of myself. This would take a bit of time. I needed a plan and soon!

Chapter 14

I felt myself soaring above the desert and I turned my feathered head to the side and saw a darker brown hawk with dark eyes at my left wing. After a short screech which I seemed to understand as a follow me, I let the hawk take the lead. I wasn't quite sure if we were going to hunt a mouse or something more intriguing. This whole night flying under the twinkling stars as a falcon was new to me, so I'd have to wait and see where this journey was taking me. I still wasn't sure if I was dreaming or if I was actually a falcon. I could hope it was a dream and worry about figuring out later.

The spotted wings ahead of me veered off to the left and headed straight down in a tailspin. Not wanting to miss out I joined the dive. The bird landed on a rock and pointed towards the entrance of a small cave. I shook my feathery head and the falcon hopped up and down bobbing her head. She screeched again giving me an imploring look. Nodding okay, I gingered put one clawed foot in front of the other. I'm not sure why I trusted this strange bird to not lead me to my doom, but for some reason I felt at ease. Ouch! My toe stubbed something hard. A hard-purple cover appeared at my feet with a blur of writing on it. I could see letters, but they swam before my eyes and seemed to be written in another language.

The other bird made a motion indicating I should take it with me, so I tried grasping it in my claws and missed. Slowly I tried again and this time I held it firmly, then we flew back.

Sunlight warmed the tent waking me up to a clatter of pots and pans making breakfast at the far end of camp. Stretching my arms above my head I felt that I was clutching something in my hand. The purple book had "Lina's journal" scrolled across the top with "top secret" written underneath it. Agape I just stared at the journal. It was true, I had flown last night. I may have been dreaming, but I carried something back with me. That's not typically how dreams work. Not only that, but this was Lina's journal. Why would the dark hawk want me to find and have this?

"Do you write?" Amy yawned.

Looking confused, I wasn't quite sure how to respond. "No, I don't. I just found this last night and thought I'd read it," I muttered.

"No need to be sarcastic. I was just wondering because I keep a journal as well. Hopefully, when I'm old and sitting in an armchair I can look back at my adventures and laugh," Amy murmured.

"First of all, you have got to break out of your shell a little to have an adventure. I saw you sneaking glances at Brian. You should ask his help today. I'm sure he'd love to talk to you," I responded with a little sass.

She giggled and got up and started getting ready. I briefly opened up the journal and saw the first entry was dated 5-12-93. Wait?! Lina's journal was started in '93. How could that be? That was like forty years ago. I just saw her last week and she was not forty. More confused I shut it, hiding it in my pillowcase, before getting up and getting ready for the day.

Breakfast was served in the tent by the time we made it up there. There was a feast of scrambled eggs, toast, and juice available. I wondered if part of tuition went to purchase supplies because I would feel horrible if we were taking away food from the tribe. Perhaps I had spoken aloud because Amy whispered, "The dig funds all our meals and also pays the tribe for our lodging so don't feel too bad about the breakfast."

My guilt assuaged for the time being, I dug in. The breakfast table talk was not nearly as chatty as it had been at dinner. Most people seemed not to be morning people and were wearing athletic clothes ready to be digging in the dirt all day. Once I was finished, I put my plate in the soak pile and began to wash the dishes that had been sitting. I was first on rotation for doing dishes, which was not a favorite of mine. Getting my hands wet with bacteria was not my idea of a good time, give me some mud any day. Seeing my discomfort, Atsa took the sponge from me and started cleaning and handed me a towel. "Here why don't you dry these and stack them up?" he said with a grin.

I smiled my gratitude and together we made quick work of the stack. As he was washing, I noticed a tattoo of a bird at his wrist and asked, "Why do you have that tattoo?"

"Oh, the hawk? That is my totem animal. It represents leadership, wisdom, and vision. I discovered this in a vision when I was a boy. Actually, your grandfather helped guide me on my vision quest," Atsa explained seriously, "So I thought to make it a permanent part of myself."

"You can turn into hawk?" my voice sounded sharp to even my ears.

Flicking a sideways look he countered, "I never said that. What makes you think that?"

"I just assumed that was how it worked, sorry," I responded nervously darting my hazel eyes away from his deep dark ones.

He shrugged and casually replied, "Only some can. It's a very special thing in deed and only those who do transform talk about it."

"Therefore, we can't talk about it?" I bantered sassily meeting his eyes.

Staring back intently, his dark eyes unblinking he said, "I don't know, can we?"

The director's voice, "Everyone get in the van. Unless you want to walk to the dig site we are leaving in a minute." Like bison everyone stampeded towards the van throwing their gear on top and the door slid closed as the last person dove in. We took off in a cloud of dust.

Upon getting to the dig site we saw an open tent with a bench and water jug sitting on it and a gridwork of holes laid out before us. The director pushed his hat further down and took off his sunglasses as he raised his clipboard up to read off a few notes. "You all know that you will be assigned a square. Make sure to dig out a layer at a time. When or if you find something, you need to mark it, tell me, then take a picture, measure where it's located, and then remove the object and put it into a bag with a label. Everyone understands how to do this, correct?" Not hearing any objections, he started calling off names and square plot numbers.

Hearing my name and the number 13, which was my lucky number, I grabbed my rucksack and gingerly climbed over the string around my excavation square. Picking up my trowel I got to work. Scrapping the digger over the top of the dirt I gently loosened it and dumped the shovelful into a bucket. I kept up this process of collecting sand and loose bits of rock until I had filled the pail. Hefting the bucket onto my shoulder I carried it down to the giant shifter and poured it through. I shook out all the sand, then examined the pieces of rock to see if any were pieces of pottery or jewelry. Archaeology could be a detailed and time-consuming task.

I kept up this task that was growing more and more monotonous by the minute. Where were the exciting things that Indy described? I saw several others shout out in victory of the finds they were discovering. Amy found a shard of pottery, a neighbor discovered a piece of jewelry, while Indy discovered some arrowheads much to his delight. Yet bucket after bucket I was only blessed with sand. I guess it was a bit naive to think that I would be out here discovering new artifacts that would change the course of history left and right. However, it seemed like everyone else had at least discovered a broken shard of pottery or something. Maybe I had a faulty dig square that no human had ever walked on before. Actually, that was kind of cool if you thought about it.

Chapter 15

A bell ringing indicated that we were done for the morning and it was time to take our lunch. Amy was passing out ham and cheese sandwiches with lettuce minus the mayo. Everyone got a sandwich, an apple, and some snack chips. It tasted like heaven to my lips despite it being a simple meal. The rest of the field crew seemed to agree as they gulped down lunch pretty quickly. The mornings exertions had left us ravenous and we quickly gobbled up everything in sight. I washed down the meal with several glasses of water, then went in search of the outdoor latrine. By outdoor latrine, I mean a scrub brush that would hide me and there weren't too many thorns in the way of crouching down.

Once I got another drink to last me until the next break, Amy asked, "You find anything yet? Or are you just being clever and keeping it to yourself for now?"

"I wish I was just being clever. No luck yet, perhaps I will fare better this afternoon," I stated glumly.

Amy frowned, "Seems odd that you can't find anything. Maybe you need to go deeper? If you don't find anything come tomorrow, I will switch your assignments if you want."

"I'd probably ruin yours as well. I'll just keep on keeping on. I might get lucky soon!" I tried to sound enthusiastic, but I could tell everyone felt horrible that I was digging up buckets and buckets of dirt, yet not hitting pay dirt so to speak. Even though we weren't treasure hunting nor did we keep the artifacts, it was just exciting to rediscover something that had been lost to times for ages.

I gave Amy my best smile and walked back kicking up dust with each step. I should've worn my boots because it felt like a ton of sand had made its home in my shoes. Shaking my shoes out before I navigated through the grid to my dig site, I hoped to feel less like a walking sandbag. Even though I felt a thin layer of silt covering me from head to toe it would be nice to have less sand stuck to me for the moment. By now my plot was dug down about fifteen inches, so I gingerly stepped down into it not wanting to knock down the wall between the plots. Thus, beginning the same process that was ongoing before lunch, dig, dump, shake, and so forth.

Pausing to wipe the sweat off my brow with a gritty hand, I left a dirt mark smear across my face which only made me look more like a failure. A hardworking failure at that. I dug my hand shovel in until it hit something hard and made a clink! Clink? Did my ears betray me? A clink meant I found something. Carefully and quickly I used my gloved hands and brushes to remove the silty dirt. Sunlight glinted off of something metallic as I removed more sand. Taking off my gloves, I gently traced the metal and ran my fingers over it trying to find the edges. Once I found where it ended I removed the rest of the sand. I wanted to grab it up and look more closely at the intricate silver piece, but knew I needed to document it properly first.

First, I grabbed the site camera and took a picture, then found my journal laying on a rock and sketched what the artifact looked like in the sand. Trying to hold in my excitement, I then used a tape measure to measure the depth it was buried and the distance from all sides of the grid to get a location for it. I recorded all this information in my journal.

At last, I was able to pick up the artifact and carefully examine it. It looked like a silver bracelet that was meant to be worn as an armband. The intricately design had a round turquoise stone streaked with veins of dark blue and black surrounded by silver feathers. Holding it I could feel myself being drawn into staring at the swirl of colors trying to see a pattern of some sort. All of a sudden, I saw an eye appear and a screech sound echoed in my ears.

"Kai, Kai! Hey looks like you found something interesting after all!" Amy's voice and shoulder shaking pulled me from the fog that had descended over me. I met her eyes and saw excitement and concern swirling there. "You okay? Did finding an artifact permanently damage you?" she joked trying to lighten the mood.

"Oh I'm fine, just excited to find something," I shyly replied.

Indy chimed in, "I think you won the pot on the most interesting find! Check out that beauty! Let me see it!"

"Sure, but don't go claiming you found it," I snickered.

Laying a hand over his heart feigning hurt he assured, "Madam I am a gentleman! I would never steal credit, you wound me."
Before long everyone had gathered around to examine the artifact and add in their two cents on how they thought it was used. Some predicted it belonged to a chief's daughter while others claimed the feathers indicated that it was used by a shaman. Our guessing was for naught because we had several tribal leaders and our lead archaeologist right on the dig site and before long they had come over to see what they

fuss was about. They took my artifact and went off to the tent to examine it further. Huddled together, they seemed to be discussing something deep, and I did begin to wonder if I had stumbled upon something more intriguing than a simple piece of jewelry. I saw Atsa look back towards me looking like he wanted to include me in the conversation, but then Yas shook his head.

"I hear that you are the person of the hour. Who'd have thought you'd make the discovery of the century? I had Indy pegged for that role, but you always do surprise me. What do you think you discovered?" Alex grumbled from behind me.

"Well don't seem too happy for me," I blurted, "Wouldn't you want me to make discoveries so the museum can keep your position?"

"Point taken. No reason to get feisty. I think they are going to assign me to help excavate the rest of your area. They are quite worried that with only one set of eyes something might be overlooked or misplaced. I told them that you were more than capable but offered to help you so you won't have to have a stranger working beside you," Alex offered.

I scoffed, "I suppose that is gallant of you." Yet, I found myself softening to him especially once we continued to dig, he offered to carry all the buckets down to shift through them. He promised if he found anything then he would have me come down. Hauling buckets and buckets all day was back breaking work so it was nice of him to offer to do it and I didn't even sense any sort of scheme. He wasn't even flirting with me, so perhaps he wasn't as bad as I thought.

Before we knew it, the director held up a megaphone and announced, "Finish up with your last shifting. The afternoon heat is getting too much. We will go back to camp and sort artifacts under the tent. Don't want to have to take anyone to the emergency room for heat stroke." His calm but deep voice echoed over the dig site. I had not made any more discoveries in my pit and the elders had taken my one find so there'd be nothing for me to sort. Either I could help someone when we got back to camp or I could read Lina's diary and perhaps figure out why I was to discover it.

I saw Alex shrug as he emptied the last bucket indicating that there was nothing in that bucket as well. I stood up and dusted myself off the best I could. Then I started to gather up my belongings and put them in my rucksack. I slung it onto my back and dumped it into the back of the van. Gulping down one last drink of water, I helped Amy carry it to the back of the van as well. Everyone was still excited from the day but was visibly exhausted. So, I sank into an empty seat on the end. I felt something crumple when I sat down. Reaching under my bottom I pulled a piece of paper from the seat. I uncrumpled it worried that someone had lost an important part of their journal. Unfurling it I read the scrawled writing, "I know what you did. You have 2 days to bring me the artifact or you are dead!"

Feeling my pulse race, I gulped nervously and made sure no one else had read the note. I wasn't quite sure what they meant but figured there would be further instructions later. Whoever was leaving me these notes was here at the dig site and could very well be in this same van with me. I couldn't trust anyone! Let alone go to anyone for help. They could very well be the crazy person or in league with them at the least!

I can see the look of fear on her face, she has no idea the source of fear is just a mere arm length away. It's hard for me to control myself around her. Do you have any idea how difficult it is to try to scare someone who is so physically close to you? Not even to mention the emotional side of things. I don't like to pat my own back or anything, but I think I deserve a medal for not being found out. It's like I'm an evil genesis mastermind. Oh yes, indeed! That is what I am! If she hasn't discovered that someone within her own close circle and camp was the one threatening her, then I doubt she will any time soon!

I could not tell if it was her ineptitude or her naivety that clouded her vision, but either way it emboldened me. I was right under her nose, yet she did not even suspect me nor anyone else close to her. I did think her brave, but now she was an easy target. She would never know that it was me leaving the notes, doll, and now even taking her most prized find on the dig today! She did not know the true value of the artifact she found, but I did. I also knew what would happen if it came up missing after she had found it.

Things were playing out perfectly into my plan. Yet, a little doubt snuck into my mind as I remembered how she had acted this morning. She had something up her sleeve, so I should take care not to underestimate her. Perhaps if I got her to trust me more, she might tell me what that is. How to earn her trust more? Make her friends look suspicious? Or perhaps play up my feelings? That could only lead to hurt for myself though. I should definitely make her feel isolated and that she can only depend on me. Perhaps, I can make her friends disappear.

Looking at my watch, I realized that I needed to meet up with my uncle and his cronies in a little bit. Hopefully, he had a better plan and one that did not involve Kai's death. For some reason he really seemed bent on revenge with her. It's not like she had disrupted his plans for the dig site, yet….

Chapter 16

After the seemingly long bumpy ride back over the pothole covered dirt road I wearily climbed out of the van unsure who to trust. I noticed Amy looking at me questioningly, but I just shook my head. Trying to avoid the others, I quickly ducked out of the group trying not to draw attention to myself. Once I was sure no one was paying attention to me I hastily headed towards my tent. Before I entered I looked behind me to make sure no one had followed me.

Once inside and out of the heat of the sun, I sat down with a huff. I had rinsed most of the dirt off myself with a wet rag before coming back, but I still took care not to sit on my sleeping bag. I hadn't quite reached the point of not caring about personal hygiene. Rummaging through my bag, my fingers grazed the leather-bound book. I had been thinking about this journal most of the day. Since I had the tent to myself now was good of time as any. I cracked open the journal and was again puzzled by the name and dates. Only reading on would quell my curiosity and solve the enigma.

As I opened the book I saw again that this book was Lina's and noted the year yet again. I had an eerie feeling tingle down my spine. A gust of wind blew sand against the tent which rocked the walls adding to the effect. Perhaps I wasn't supposed to be reading this and went to close it. Then, I noticed the wind picked up even more. Cautiously, I flipped to the next page and the wind stopped. Shrugging my shoulders, I started to read the journal.

3-12-93
Today father informed me that I would be helping the Americorps volunteers and some archaeologists who were coming out in a few weeks. I can't believe Ahiga would subject me to such torture! He knows I want to go to Washington D.C. and become a lawyer for the Nation. I would much rather do a summer internship in Albuquerque. The spring cacti flowers are less wilted than my dreams and they have been curled since spring!

Maybe I can talk some sense into him. These people coming won't help us, they care little and just want a summer of adventure. Although, father claims that I can do my duty to my people best by being diplomatic. He said, "Learning to work together with these people and showing the world what great things, we accomplish is the surest way to reach peace and prosperity." He may have also stated that it would teach me patience and humbleness.

I know he did great things for our country and our tribe by being a code talker, but he didn't realize that times were different now. There were marches on Washington demanding change. Between the Civil Rights and

Women's Rights movements now was the time to fight for our rights.

Ahiga? Was Lina an aunt of sorts? That was my grandfather. How could it be that he was her father? No one told me that my mother had a sister! I looked up from the journal contemplatively. Perhaps at dinner I would ask Atsa. I'm sure he would be willing to help me discover my family and wouldn't seem suspicious of my questions. For some reason Yas seemed more closed off about answering such things. While welcoming, he has put up a sort of wall. Glancing at my watch I saw that I had a bit more time before we would start getting things ready for dinner.

3-26-93

I have been so busy getting everything ready for our visitors. I had no idea that I would need to set up some temporary shelter, get contacts with the other small villages, and get food. My father has been helpful in finding volunteers. It seems like no one can deny him anything when he asks and that includes myself.

I also have been exchanging several letters with this man, Clay. He claims to have an interest in Navajo history and wanting to use the past to help fuel present help. I sort of wrote him off, but he's very adamant about coming out this summer. We shall see how much help he is when he gets out here. Although, Ahiga claims that the man already raised close to 100,000 dollars to fund a dig site and start a well. The man must be an idiot wanting to build wells in the desert. Does he plan to store up all the cacti water?

I was actually looking forward to watching this awkward man try to survive in the desert. Perhaps I could prank him a bit.

4-02-93

Well I will say that Clay man is quite maddening even if his mossy green eyes are hypnotic. He acts like he knows everything and is so nice and polite it makes you want to punch him in the face. He even has my father under his spell and has his respect which is something that is hard to earn.

It was going to be an interesting summer.

Although, I will say his friend, Nikkoli, is quite odd. He claims to be a geologist with an interest in well drilling, but he gives me the creeps. I can't quite put my finger on it, but something is up with him.

Well whatever I had found was interesting to say the least. This must have been when the dig first got started. I closed the book and bounded off in the heat of the sun to get some answers.

"Hey where have you been? I heard from someone that you were burying your hidden treasure. That seems like an odd rumor to come about, but I haven't seen you since we got out of the van," Amy accused.

"Who said I was burying treasure?" I looked up appalled, "I was just journaling like you saw me this morning."

Amy looked embarrassed and whispered, "Oh just some gossip going around camp. I should've known better than to believe it. Just seemed odd that you just up and disappeared. Let me know next time, I'll cover for you."

Seeing Atsa come into the dining tent, I told Amy that I needed to talk to him and made my way over. He was talking to a few of the elders when I came up behind him and asked, "Hey, do you have a minute?" He nodded and excused himself to follow me over to the far side of the tent. Once we were away from the others I asked, "Did my cousin ever mention an aunt I might have?"

Atsa looked very confused and said, "You only have two uncles as far as I know. We really do need to get you out to see Ahiga when your cousin gets back tomorrow. Why do you ask?"

"Oh I found this journal the other day and it said Lina on it and I'm assuming it's my aunt's because she keeps referring to Ahiga being her father," I began.

"You found Lina's journal? Where did you find it? Forget dinner, I am going to drive you to Ahiga's now!" Atsa insisted.

Feeling rushed and confused, I felt Atsa pull on my arm while I planted my feet. "I'm not going anywhere until you tell me what is going on! You are starting to scare me!" I shouted with a quivering voice. Just then Alex appeared by my side and demanded to know what was going on. I couldn't help but lean into him a little bit. For several minutes it was like chaos had broken loose and the two men were shouting over each other. I couldn't understand much, but they were drawing quite a crowd and I was completely embarrassed.

Just then Johanna entered the tent and pushed the two men apart. "Now somebody tell me exactly what is going on here!" Relief washed over me seeing my cousin. I could tell her what was going on and she would find a way to fix things.

"He has no business in any of this!" Atsa pointed at Alex, "He is not one of us. I told him to stay out of our issues. I still hear stories about the last time the tribe trusted an outsider."

"I was just trying to protect Kai. She was very upset and he was pushing her around! He's a maniac!" Alex growled defensively.

"He's not a maniac. I just wanted his help with something, now I'm not quite ready to face it. That's all. Can I talk with you privately Johanna? Away from all this chaos," I pleaded.

She nodded and gently maneuvered me through crowd and outside. Once we were outside, the floodgates opened and I spilled all the secrets that I had been keeping. I told her about the falcon dreams, the museum, and most recently the journal. The more I told her the wider her eyes became. "You found Lina's journal?" she gasped.

"Yes, but in an odd sort of way. I don't actually remember getting it, but I dreamed about finding it yet and voila there it is!" I exclaimed. "I know this is all sort of crazy, but I want to know what is happening to me and why I found this journal!"

"Let's go visit Ahiga. Our grandfather might be able to help with this more," she replied calmly.

She led me over to her jeep and we got in. It was still daylight and I enjoyed feeling the air whip through my long hair. The feeling calmed my nerves and I felt myself begin to relax. Johanna gave me a reassuring smile and squeezed my shoulder in support. I was glad to have the burden of my secret of my chest; however, I still wished to have answers and was hoping to get them soon. Staring off into the endless desert, I began to see a mirage that slowly transformed into a house.

Now was the perfect time for stage two of my plan. The events could not have aligned themselves better and almost seemed predetermined that I should continue scheme to frame Kai. She looked so suspicious right now anyways. Running off into the night with a virtual stranger, fighting publicly, and carrying on like a banshee all made her look certifiable and unbelievable if she were to deny any charges. In fact, it appeared she might even believe that she did do herself.

I blended into the crowd and faded into the twilight. Everyone seemed to be busy gossiping and trying to figure out what was wrong with Kai. No one was even guarding the tent that held the more important artifacts. Quietly, I made my way over to the tent trying to stay to the outskirts of camp and lurking behind tents and sagebrush clumps. I heard a noise and backed up quickly right into a prickly bush. I had to clamp a hand over my mouth to keep from drawing attention with a curse or scream. Seeing a rabbit hop off I cursed at myself for being so jumpy over a silly rabbit.

Finally, I was beside the tent and the artifacts were within my grasp. With efficient hands I pulled back the tent flap and scanned the area. Seeing the turquoise jewelry laying out, I nervously bit my lip and grabbed them up. Gently, I stuck as much as I could carry easily into my pockets and jacket. Once finished I ducked out of the tent looking to my left, then right ensuring that no one was watching.

Subsequently, I headed towards Kai's tent to execute the framing part of my plan. Weaving my way through the camp like a snake I saw a few people walking around and tried to look inconspicuous. Looking up at the night sky, I pretended to study the stars pointing at constellations for effect. Hearing the voices drift off I snuck into Kai's tent and quickly put the artifact under her pillow.

Oomph! I ran into something solid, but human. "Hey what are you doing here?" Crap! I had run into her roommate. Briefly, I debated knocking her over the head. Framing her for theft and murder would really nail her coffin shut, but I had never hurt anyone physically and wasn't sure I could actually do it. Plus, hiding the body could be difficult.

"Oh, I was just going to check on Kai. She seemed upset. Since she isn't here, I just left her a note," I smiled my most charming smile which seemed to convince her.

Breathing in a sigh of relief, I went off to meet my fence who would buy the rest of my loot and sell it to others interested in collecting. The quicker I got rid of these stolen items, the better. I could ruin my plot otherwise.

Chapter 17

Hearing the gravel crunch under the tires as we screeched to a stop, I saw the flickering porch light beside the door as it opened up. Johanna smiled and waved. My fingers shook as I went to open the door. I was about to meet my grandfather for the first time. What if he hated me? I shuffled through the sand with my eyes downcast worried that he was disappointed I had never attempted to meet him. How could he know that I never knew he existed? Perhaps he could have come to visit me, or he might have been in the dark all this time just like me.

Before I knew it, I was enveloped in a warm hug that smelled vaguely of pipe tobacco. "Welcome my child. Come tell me what ails you," Ahiga said in a strong assured voice. Looking up into his face I could see that I had his long strong nose and immediately felt a connection.

With a quavering hand that I tried to steady I handed over Lina's journal. I saw the look of shock on his face when he whispered, "Where did you find your mother's journal?"

"My mother?" I blurted.

"Yes, your mother's name was Lina. Did you not know, child? I know she often went by your father's nickname for her, Eagle, because she enjoyed his teasing," Ahiga murmured, "I didn't know your uncle was so cold hearted to not tell you. I should've come for you even when he told me it was too soon."

There was so much I did not know. I tried to fight the feelings of betrayal from all sides. I knew that they had made mistakes, but hopefully both my uncle and grandfather did so to keep me safe. If I found out otherwise, then I would not be so forgiving. So instead of lashing out I asked him to explain. "Could you tell me more about my mother?"

"Your mother's name was Lina as you now know. Shortly after she fell in love with your father they married and had you. Unfortunately, one day they were out on the dig site and that was the last time we ever say them. They had left you with me and when they did not return that night to get you. I knew something was wrong. I could feel it. These feelings are hard to explain, but perhaps you know what I speak of," he said with a solemn look that seared into my very soul, "Anyways, when your mother did not return we assembled a search party. The only thing we ever found was their van broken down along the road. It appeared to have a bullet hole in the tire and a window. No blood, bullets, or bodies were ever found."

"Is that it? Didn't the police or someone try to find evidence?" I asked trying to hold in my outrage.

"A week or so later the police received a postcard from Mexico saying how your parents had run off to escape their problems.

They called off the investigation. I was too poor and embarrassed at the time to look into it more. I wish I would've because I know in my heart that my daughter did not run off and abandon her daughter. She loved you just as much as she loved fighting for what was right," Ahiga sighed in shame.

I put my hand on his shoulder and squeezed saying, "The fault is not yours. The police should've investigated more. Did they ever find any plane tickets or anything to indicate that they did leave?"

"Not that I am aware. I did know something though and never mentioned it. She came to me before she disappeared and talked about a certain artifact. Someone wanted it she claimed. Yet, no artifacts came up missing and shortly after the dig site was abandoned. Then several years later an oil company approached us, but when we told them we did not want to lease our land the idea was forgotten as well. I could never make any connection. I was quite a wreck having just lost my youngest daughter. Especially, since your father's brother showed up with a will that said you needed to go live with them. I didn't fight it and knew you would have a better life with them. I just never knew you would never know your own mother!" Ahiga seemed pained as he explained with a voice thick with emotion. Tears gathered in the wrinkles surrounding his dark eyes.

Stunned I looked at my cousin and grandfather and replied, "So my mother is either living in Mexico or something else happened? Do you have a picture of her when she was my age?"

"Yes, let me find one," Ahiga murmured.

"Where did you say you found her journal?" Johanna asked with a hint of concern and suspicion in her voice.

"It's a long story…" I began. Gasping I saw the picture that grandfather's picture of my mother. "Oh my gosh! Her eyes are the same! That's Lina!"

"Of course, it's your mother," responded Ahiga in a confused tone.

"No, I saw her earlier this summer! She was my partner at the museum," I sputtered.

My grandfather and cousin exchanged a knowing look and my cousin motioned for me to have a seat in a yellow age worn recliner. With a reassuring hand on my shoulder she urged, "Why don't you start at the beginning? We are here to help. Nothing you will say could shock us."

"Yes, I have seen it all on the battlefields during WWII and all the years as a shaman. I have walked with the skin walkers, and helped those find their spiritual path," Ahiga added with a slight twinkle in his eye showing his humorous side.

For some reason this put me at ease. Taking a deep breath, I took in my surroundings. Ahiga's house felt familiar and seemed like a window to the past. A woven blanket full of colors hung on the wall above the couch, beside it was a phone with the old rotary turn dial also the color of golden rod. The room was sparsely lit with a few dusty lamps giving it a warm cozy feel. Burnt pipe tobacco hung lightly in the air smelling slightly sweet and tickling my nostrils.

Breathing in the comfort I began at the start of the summer. I told them about how I met Lina and how someone took our artifacts. I was recounting events, I started to see them differently. I realized that anytime I was with Lina, people were talking to me, and no one seemed to notice her. It began to hit me that perhaps that I was the only one who saw her. Stumbling a bit over my story, I continued to tell them how someone followed me. Then hesitating even more, I slowly started to tell them how I witnessed the museum break in where several important artifacts were stolen.

"How were you in the museum so late?" Johanna pondered out loud.

"Well I wasn't quite there. I dreamed I was there, but in my dream, I was a falcon. I heard the artifacts talking to me, heard people come in and take them while I was able to escape out a window. However, I woke up in bed as a human. It's a little confusing. The same thing happened when I found Lina's journal. In my dream I was following another darker falcon or hawk. Sadly, I'm not quite sure of the differences as I never studied birds," I paused.

"Go on. I know this seems strange and crazy, but I promise you aren't alone. You will find out soon enough that there are others like you, but first I want to hear the rest of your story," Ahiga encouraged.

Nodding I continued, "The other falcon seemed to be talking to me and wanted me to follow. The falcon led me through the desert at night and to a cave. It seemed to want me to go inside and for some crazy reason I listened. That's where I found the journal. Then, when I woke up I was holding the journal. At that time, I wasn't quite sure whose it was and I have just started reading it."

"I'm going to make a phone call. I think that he might be able to help," Johanna stated.

"Who can help?" I asked.

Chapter 18

Johanna opened the old creaky door as it let out a long sigh and something flew through kitchen. A falcon landed on the chair and I looked puzzled to my grandfather. He just motioned back to the bird where it was shaking it's feathers almost like it was trying to shake off its skin. Slowly before my eyes I witnessed the falcon transform into Atsa and my jaw dropped to the floor in disbelief.

"Atsa?!" I cried.

"Yes, he is a student of mine. Sadly, the transformation takes too much out of me these days. Generally, skin walkers have a bad reputation, however some of us have the ability and use it for good and not evil. When Atsa discovered his ability, he came to me as a boy and I have kept him from following the path of evil," Ahiga explained.

"I was just as scared as you are when I found out. Don't worry having help with the process will make it easier. You aren't alone and you aren't making up things in your head, I promise. It sure felt that way on several occasions," Atsa commented.

The daylight faded into dusk as we discussed when we learned of our abilities and why we had them. Ahiga had made some tea and shared the tragic legend of the first skin walker. He had killed his family and donned the skin of a coyote to escape notice and was forever banished. Since then some of his descendants have the ability to shapeshift. Unfortunately, many use this ability for bad, but if done correctly you don't have to worry about slipping into the darkness.

Feeling a little overwhelmed, but more knowledgeable about the situation I told everyone that I was getting a bit tired and wanted to sleep on everything I had just learned.

Atsa offered, "Would you like me to escort you back? You can try to control your shapeshifting and fly with me."

I hesitated, then agreed since it would be nice to have control over this power instead of it controlling me. I nodded my agreement and he carefully walked me through it.

"Flap your arms," he instructed and when I did so, he burst out laughing. I gave him a glare and he continued, "Sorry, I couldn't resist. Can you blame me? First close your eyes and envision yourself soaring, then picture where it is you want to go. This time I'm serious."

I closed my eyes and pictures clouds and blue sky all around me with a painted desert soaring by under me. The next thing I knew I felt myself lift up as feathers appeared on my arms and I slowly shrank into a falcon. Before my eyes I saw my feet curl up into claws. Bump! I winced as I hit my head on the ceiling of the house. I looked down and saw the three of them smiling up at me. Then, Atsa started to make the change as well. With his eyes closed I saw feathers appear in place of his hair, then his arms as he grew smaller. His face narrowed into a sharper look as his nose transformed into a beak. He too started to fly half human and half hawk until he made his transformation complete. It was quite a sight to see and I would've been scared had I not been surrounded by caring people easing me into it.

Flapping my wings to keep my afloat I started to become more aware of myself as a bird. I had keener vision and was able to spot the slightest movement and very acute hearing. If I paid attention I could almost hear the heartbeat of both Ahiga and Johanna. Feeling a sensory overload coming on I stopped experimenting. Instead I concentrated on trying to gain some more control over my flying as Atsa was trying to show me how to do some tricks. I wasn't quite up to that yet and ignored his more difficult maneuvers.

Once I felt comfortable in my new skin I screeched at Atsa who took off out the door expecting me to follow. I hoped I had said, "Let's go back to camp." However, considering I was still a little new to all of this I was not quite sure what I had said. He led me swooping over the dark desert. Screeching he flew in a circle indicating that I needed to look down. I saw a mouse scurrying around and trying to hide in a hole dug into a cactus. Poor thing probably thought we were hunting. Luckily for it I had already eaten. I could also see some bats swooping around trying to capture a scorpion. From up above it looked like they were dancing, but it was a dance of death. If the scorpion could not ward off the bat with its poisonous bard, then it was doomed to be eaten alive. Perhaps the animal world was more gruesome and dangerous than the human one. I thought, "Falcons don't really have any natural enemies." I really hoped that was the case anyways.

I caught a wind wave and caught up to Atsa soaring along beside him under the blanket of stars. He turned his head towards me and seemed to smile as he did a barrel roll to stare up at me upside down. I laughed at his silliness glad that he was making this feel less peculiar. While it still felt a little strange it was nice to know I wasn't a lone freak.

After what seemed like hours but was only minutes we spotted the camp with a rock cliff at its edge rising high into the night sky. A fire's embers glowed below in the middle of camp and tents fanned out in all directions. It was quite late and most of the lights were out indicating most of the people were probably asleep. Atsa motioned for me to follow him to the edge of camp behind a clump of bushes. There we perched on the ground and I watched Atsa start the transformation process first. His feathers seeming to disappear into his arms and head as hair instead of fluff.

Within a few minutes he was towering over me as a man again with almost no trace of falcon left except for the feather hanging in his long shaggy dark hair. He shook his head and it fell to the ground as I stood a little mesmerized by the sight of him. I waited a moment and yet I did not make the transformation. I closed my eyes and concentrated even holding my breath. Yet, again nothing occurred. As if sensing my confusion Atsa looked at me and said, "You have to visualize being human again. Try thinking about walking or swimming."

I squeezed my eyes shut yet visualizing walking did nothing. However, this time I imagined Atsa taking me into his arms and kissing me deeply. That must have done it because all of a sudden, I started to turn back into a human. I could feel my skin stretching as I grew and my body tingled where the feathers seemed to pull back inside my skin and the joints in my wings returned to elbows and wrists. Once all my falcon features were gone, I felt my falcon senses slip away and was quite surprised that within minutes I felt like a normal human again.

Atsa smiled and gave me a quick hug before he whispered, "Uh goodnight. We can try the shapeshifter thing some more. You'll get the hang of it. Don't worry you aren't alone. I should probably get back home, I can only miss curfew so many times." He smiled ruefully and transformed back into a falcon to take off into the night.

Trying not to be too entranced I watched him fly off for a second, then shook myself for being silly. I'm sure Atsa had plenty of girls drooling over him and I didn't need to be his summer fling. He was turning into a good friend and that's how I should keep it.

Turning back towards camp, I hiked back through the scrub brush trying not get any thorns stuck in my clothes or my legs. My feet left dusty footprints as I shuffled quietly back to my tent. I had thought about smudging them away, but that would keep me out longer making me even more suspicious. So, I quickly made my way through the darkness trying not to trip over rocks or tent posts until I came to my tent. Before I unzipped the tent to enter, I quickly fabricated a story to tell Amy if she were to ask why I was up so late. Taking a deep breath, I entered and pulled back the covers to my cot and climbed in. Through the darkness I heard Amy mumble, "Where have you been?"

"Oh, I just went to meet my grandfather and go back a little late," I deliberately left out the details, "I will tell you about it tomorrow. I am beat."

I heard her mumble okay. Forgetting all about wanting to read my mother's journal I fell into a deep sleep. The most restful and peaceful sleep I had since I started this adventure. Not once dreaming of a falcon or missing artifacts.

I watched her come out of the desert night with that trickster. Had she snuck off with him the whole night? I'm not sure why I cared, but I did. I wanted to make them both pay and not just because it was my job anymore. They were up to something. What, I was not sure. If they were trying to make a fool out of me, then they would be the fools.

Either way it was just making my plan that much easier. Sadly, she was going to end up like her mother if she was not careful. I remember hearing stories about her and how she had gotten in the way as well. Looks like it was time to watch my plan unfold in the morning. Perhaps, I would even ask to see the artifacts earlier to get her out of here even more quickly.

I really did need to figure out what her secrets were though before they cost me everything I had worked hard to achieve.

Chapter 19

With the desert sun rays filtering through the tent I awoke to a yellow haze throughout the tent. Giving it a surreal feel. Slowly I was feeling more comfortable with myself and accepting what I was. I was ready to find out more about my mom and myself today. Wishing to read more of my mother's journal I dug around in my sleeping bag for it. I figured I had at least an hour before others woke up to get breakfast. I settled in trying not to disturb Amy.

5-12-93

I haven't had much time for writing because we have been very busy at the dig site. We haven't made any discoveries yet, but it takes quite a bit to set up the area. After mapping out a grid we did several shovel tests only to find that we were off on our area. So we had to start the process over again several times.

This whole time Clay has been very helpful. I was worried about bringing in a buffoon, but he seems quite intelligent. He listens to the elders, but he is also trying to use some new technology to determine where additional ruins may be. He is even very helpful by getting extra funding to dig the community some new wells which will occur later in the year. While I still distrust his friend Nikkoli, he seems to want to help us find some sources of water.

5-28-93

It's been quite a busy month as we have discovered several sites and Nikkoli has begun to at least find some water sources. He claims that it will be quite awhile until he can drill a well. His geology skills have come in quite handy.

I'm also kind of excited because after our last date Clay took me for a walk under the stars and he told me that he loved me. Who knew he'd crack this stubborn heart of mine? He wants us to work together both on the reservation and in Washington D.C. He's encouraging me to get my law degree and has some grand ideas about turning the dig site into a tourist attraction. At first the elders were opposed to this idea, but after hearing Clay's argument they agreed. He said that I would draw up the papers that they would be the majority vote on everything with the dig and museum. They would have control over what they wanted to display and all the money would go to the reservation. I can't believe such a man exists especially since he is an outsider.

6-04-93

More exciting news! Clay has asked me to marry him and even though my father is a little grumpy he gave his approval. We are planning to elope to Vegas soon. We didn't want to plan a fancy wedding. I'm a little nervous but can't wait. I am debating about telling him about my

abilities, but he may not understand. Perhaps, I will tell him later.

Does this mean that my mother was also a shape shifter? I was also quite shocked that my mother was planning to elope with my father. They had quite the whirlwind romance it seemed. Sadly, it seemed to have ended just as tragically as Romeo and Juliet. There was some question as to whether or not they were dead, but highly doubted that they dumped me to live the good life in Mexico. If nothing else both of my parents seemed dedicated to their work. I tended to agree with Ahiga that they were no longer alive.

This thought saddened me since I never got to know them. I must get my passionate nature and work habits from them. My mother sort of reminded me of myself and actually reminded me of Lina. Then all of a sudden it hit me. If Lina was my mom's name and she looked like the picture, then the Lina I knew in Washington was probably my mother! I wonder why her spirit appeared to me? The pieces of the puzzle began to fall into place. I bet the falcon that appeared in my dreams was her as well? Could she come back and tell me more? It felt so odd to have been so close to her, yet not know how close she was to me. It was almost comical that all of this was happening to me since I never really believed in ghosts, spirits, or anything supernatural. I always thought I was rational, but it was rather hard to deny that I had seen a ghost of my mother and I did transform into a falcon. Wanting to know more I continued reading.

6-22-93

We just got back from our wedding and short honeymoon. I have been so happy, but I am starting to get the dreams again. I worry that I should tell Clay my suspicions, but what if he rejects who I am at my core.

Especially now that I think I may be pregnant. I hope he would be understanding, but I can only imagine how an outsider would feel about having a half human baby.

6-29-93

I told Clay that I was worried that there would be a heist at the dig site. I was so happy when he believed me but was a bit worried when I had to explain my reasons. He had Nikkoli set up security at the dig site at night, but I still had a funny feeling. I really wanted to transform and keep an eye on things at night. However, I was worried the transformation would hurt the baby so I resisted.

7-10-93

I was right! We aren't even sure what all was stolen, but several items we dug up were taken. There were also big holes throughout the site indicating that the thieves also tried to find new artifacts to plunder. I was so upset and blamed Nikkoli, but Clay pointed out that he had been attacked and was unconscious the whole time. I took to my bed for days not wanting to talk with anyone. I was so upset that I even threw up several times. Clay was so supportive and was extremely worried about me. He has been on a mission to find out who was responsible. He called in local and federal authorities, but so far, they have found nothing.

7-15-93

I have even more sad news. Not only did they not find those responsible, but the elders want to shut down the dig for the summer. I know that I will not rest until I get to the bottom of this….

Ahem! A coughing sound caused me to look up from my mother's journal. I saw Amy sitting up watching me with a frown. Curiously, I tilted my head questionably wondering why she was watching me so intently. "Where did you go last night? I didn't even hear you come in," her voice sounded accusing to my ears.

"I just went to see my grandfather. There's some stuff going on, you wouldn't understand," I explained.

She narrowed her eyes and replied, "Perhaps if you would explain it to me, I would understand. Fine keep your secrets. I'm sure I can't help anyways since I don't understand anything." She got up angrily and got ready for the day, then looked ready to stomp out of the tent.

"Amy, wait… I'm sorry. Sit down," I sighed feeling like I had hurt her, but also anxious about exposing too much. What if she told everyone else? Or she thought I was a freak or crazy? She was my only friend here at the dig, but I feared if I didn't open up to her I would still lose her as a friend.

She turned and waited by the edge of the tent. Seeing my serious expression her own expression softened and she touched my arm and said, "If this is hard for you, you can tell me later. I just worry that you are in trouble." When I just stuttered and didn't respond she looked back at me sadly and slipped out of the tent. Ugh why did this have to be so hard? I was beginning to miss my normal life in Boulder where I went hiking with friends, I wondered about my past and felt like something was missing. Well I had found out what was missing and now I just felt more confused and alone.

I got ready and made my way to the breakfast tent. I bumped into Alex on the way who seemed genuinely concerned and asked if I was alright. I nodded and tried to brush past him, but he put his arms around me. I stared down at his blue sneakers and didn't hug him back and could feel Atsa's eyes on my back. I pulled away and Alex told me, "Sorry, I was just worried. You disappeared last night and was just glad you made it back. You never know what can happen at night." He said this fairly loudly causing everyone around us to turn and give me a questioning glance. I couldn't help but feel like everyone was accusing me of something.

Ahhhhh! The dig director came bursting into the tent in a panic. Everyone was looking around to see what was chasing him, but it was just him. He headed over to the elders in the corner of the tent, then accidentally shouted, "They've taken it!" Everyone's heads whipped around to see who had taken what. The crowd inside of the tent quickly turned to chaos with everyone whispering their ideas as to what was going on. I heard someone whisper, "I bet it's that girl. She was gone, now things are missing." Then others said, "He probably misplaced the artifacts, he's kind of an idiot at times. Did you see him yesterday? Plus, he is acting way out of control right now. He should've been watching them more closely."

I inched my way closer trying to hear what was going on when I became aware of Atsa to my left. He whispered, "Don't worry, we have come up with an alibi for you and you won't be seriously accused. Are you feeling better this morning? Did you sleep ok?"

"Like a baby bird," I replied offhandedly watching the scene around me unfold, "Do you know what's going on?"

"The artifacts were stolen right out of the tent!" everyone heard the director shout and we all grew quiet waiting for him to explain. He seemed surprised that others had heard and that we were waiting with baited breath to hear what else he had to say. He pulled up a little straighter, "As many of you might have heard the artifacts that were uncovered yesterday are not where they are supposed to be and are missing. If anyone knows anything about their whereabouts or if you saw anything please see me."

"It seems that there were a lot of strange things happening last night," Atsa whispered to me.

"You should check all of the tents," announced Alex.

We all looked over towards him at his suggestion. Was he implying that one of us took the artifacts? I'm pretty sure we were all here because we wanted to study history, not steal it. Yet, I remembered that he was probably just doing his job. He wasn't trying to throw us under the bus, but just research all the possibilities.

Chapter 20

Wanting to keep the day as normal as possible the director had ushered us all into the van to the dig site. There were whispers that they just wanted to be able to search our tents in secret, but I wasn't worried about any of that. Besides, I had tucked my mother's journal into my satchel to read later on today. Her diary was the only thing that I worried about others finding since it had our shared secret and ability. I took a bite of the cereal bar on the ride out. I was glad I had taken the bar and the apple from the buffet since I had almost missed breakfast with all the excitement this morning.

Looking back towards camp, I saw a falcon circling above what looked to be my tent. Diving gracefully, it floated through the open flap easily and unnoticed by everyone but me. It didn't look like Atsa and I puzzled over this a minute thinking perhaps it was a random bird. The memory of the falcon flooded back into my mind hitting me like a ton of bricks. It was the falcon from my dream! Wonder what it was doing in my tent of all places? Was it bringing me more clues?

Alex elbowed me in the side, "What are you thinking about? You seemed in another world."

"Oh I was for a moment," I returned with a grin.

He didn't seem to know what to make of that and went back to watching the landscape. His phone kept going off and I asked him if he was going to answer it. He shook his head and grunted, "Oh just some telemarketers that won't stop pestering me, I'll return their call later. Besides we are about to leave cell phone service here soon."

An occasional pot hole or rough pavement would jostle the van tossing me into his side and I couldn't help but notice Atsa glowering in the front seat. Could it be that he was jealous of Alex? I saw Alex more like a colleague and Atsa was a close friend who made my heart race, but he didn't need to know that yet. Besides, how would that work? I didn't see Atsa wanting to move to Washington D.C. or to Colorado. I'm not quite why I was mapping out our possible futures when I wasn't even sure if he liked me that way. I should just concentrate on figuring out what happened to my mother and what was happening to me. Perhaps she turned into a falcon and never returned. I made a mental note to ask if that was even possible.

After a thought provoking van ride under a bright clear turquoise sky with hardly a cloud to provide shelter from the sizzling sun. I pulled the bill of my hat further down shielding my eyes from the brightness as I exited the van. By now most of us knew what we were supposed to do and we filed through the dig site like worker ants doing our assigned jobs. Most of us were assigned a grid plot to excavate while some were busy sorting and labeling the uncovered artifacts.

Within no time, I had found a rhythm in the almost mindless work of excavating. Dig, scoop, shift. Dig, scoop, shift. Occasionally, while shifting the dirt I found trivial broken pieces that would've been exciting yesterday, but now were nothing notable. I still bagged and tagged them since they could provide more valuable information in a lab analysis. Generally, the already broken up pieces were examined under microscopes and tested to determine when they were made and if there were any chemical markers. Archaeology while a seemingly archaic practice with the digging and dirt, it was a very technologically advanced field as well. Staring at the shard, I wondered what the Lab scientists could unravel about this mysterious piece. Maybe with chemical analysis they could even determine the types of food that were stored inside. At least I had read about them being able to do this. I would love to visit a lab and see this first hand, but I needed much more training in chemistry first.

Putting the shard away, I got back to my digging before anyone noticed me waxing poetically about a bit of ancient clay. Indy could get away with that sort of behavior, but I wanted to be taken a bit more seriously. Continuing with my work, it did not take long before I had to climb out of the hole I had dug myself into. It seems that I was a bit quicker with this process than I had anticipated when I heard the cry, "Lunch break!" I dusted myself off the best I could, then tried to climb out only to have a hand on the other side grab mine and help pull me up. The warm dark hand sent a shiver up my spine, and I knew that it was Atsa before I even looked into his dark eyes. Smiling shyly, I thanked him and tried not to blush.

Seeing them together made me sick. I looked up from my digging and there they were. Ignoring them, I shifted through the sand to find another artifact. Staring at the shiny turquoise, I was mesmerized. Since I was already breaking the law, there didn't seem to be any harm in taking something for myself. I was keeping my sister safe with this mission, but I wasn't exactly getting paid. So why not take a little something for myself? Maybe I could start a new life with my sister away from my uncle, perhaps even Kai could come along. The idea made me happy.

Atsa followed me through the lunch line as I picked up a ham and cheese sandwich from the cooler. I added some bbq chips and an apple to my plate before I grabbed a cup of water. Sitting down beside Amy at the picnic table, I noticed that Atsa sat on the other side. "How is your grid going? Find anything interesting?" I asked Amy. She still seemed mad, but her tone suggested she was trying to be cordial.

I took a drink then replied, "Oh I'm digging myself into a pit, but mostly I am finding dust. A few pieces of pottery, but nothing near as exciting as yesterday. How about you?"

"I did find a scorpion while digging earlier this morning, but I brushed it into a shovel and carried it over to the brush to release it. Other than that, not even a pottery piece. Perhaps the dig site is cursed and there is nothing to find," Amy stated.

"What makes you think it's cursed?" I inquired curiously wondering what she had heard and from whom.

Amy's deep blue eyes met my hazel gaze as she nodded her head in Indy's direction, "Last night when you vanished, Indy told everyone a story that he had heard. He claimed that some locals had warned him that the dig site was cursed and sometimes they heard creepy ghoulish screeching and howling during the darkest part of the night."

"Yes, they have even had people disappear or so I've heard. Along with shadows that dance when there is no light from the moon," Alex's voice interrupted Amy's as he shot her a wicked grin. He was continuing to the tell the story that he had told us from the first day and spreading it around camp apparently.

Atsa rolled his eyes and sighed, "All of that nonsense is just a bunch of hokum we tell the tourists to keep them out of the dig at night. If we really wanted to share our secrets we would tell them the legend of the skin walkers. Or even show them."

"Either way I wouldn't want to be left here at night by myself," Alex urged.

"Me either! I don't plan on missing the bus ever. You could be eaten by a coyote let alone be stuck with any of the ghosts," Amy agreed.

Looking back and forth between Amy and Alex, I wondered if there was something going on between them. Perhaps, I should share more with Amy so she didn't feel so left out. I made me a mental note to show her my mother's diary later that afternoon once everyone else got back to work. I didn't want her and Alex getting too close. It was just a strange feeling and I couldn't really pinpoint why I felt that way.

Hearing the bell ring, we all knew it was time to finish up and get back to work. Morning was an enjoyable time to work, but the afternoon was grueling work. My skin prickled as I already felt the sweat start to trickle down my back. As I walked back with Amy, Atsa took me aside and whispered, "I'm going to head back by way of the sky to check on your grandfather and see what has been happening back at camp. If you need anything don't hesitate to meet me in the sky. Watch your back, I don't trust some of your classmates."

Nodding, I tucked his advice away for later use. Perhaps he had a feeling something would happen later. I didn't get quite get vibes, but I did trust those who did. One of my Instagram friends, Zoe, used her telepathic abilities and vibes to find criminals. I always followed her adventures and blog because it was cool that a teenager was doing something so awesome. Maybe I should message her to see if she could see anything about my mother's diary, I thought and made a mental note to remember to facetime her later if we had internet access.

Amy's voice drifted in and interrupted my thoughts pulling me back into this world. "Are you ready to talk about last night? I really want to believe you, but others are talking about how suspicious it is that you departed last night and this morning someone absconded with the artifacts. Let me help you," she implored her eyes shone with emotion.

"Meet me in my grid in about 30 minutes and I will show you what I was doing last night. I could use some insight especially from an outsider's perspective. It's kind of weird, I want to prepare you, so if you aren't up for something odd, then don't come," I warned hoping that she would show up. It would be nice to not have any more secrets. Secrets could eat you alive.

Chapter 21

Pebbles tumbled into my hole in the sand from above along with a clump of red sand stuck to a sneaker. Guessing it was Amy coming to join me, I crawled to the opposite wall so that she wouldn't accidentally step on me. Once she was in all the way down I asked, "Did you tell anyone you or did anyone see you?" in a hushed voice.

"Relax 007, no one saw. Even if they did, they would just assume we were comparing artifacts," she said rolling her eyes.

"You'll see why I want it secret in a minute," as I pulled out my mother's journal, "This is what I have been hiding. I found it the other day and just discovered that it was my mother's and I am fairly certain she was murdered because of what's in here," I said passionately.

"Murdered? Recently? Was the journal at the dig?" Amy spewed out questions right and left.

Calmly, I held up a finger to my lips to silence her then pointed up. Showing her that I didn't want everyone else to overhear us. Then I started my story at the beginning sharing with her how I found the journal, the museum, and how I could shapeshift. As I was babbled on revealing all my secrets, I was worried that this was too much, but as I looked up I saw a look of understanding cross her face. Amy seemed to believe my story and she did not interrupt me once. I was so relieved because honestly, I wasn't quite so sure I believed myself and I was living it.

She reached out a hand to lay on my arm comforting me and I couldn't hold back a sob as it choked out of me. My strong resolve that I had been holding back, burst like a dam letting out a flood of emotions. "Hey it's okay. I believe you. Truthfully, it's all so crazy it's difficult to think you would actually make that up. We should read more of your mother's journal to see if we can come up with some answers or return to where you found it if nothing else to see if there are any clues there," Amy insisted, "I want to help you solve this."

Smiling brightly, I hugged her briefly before I said, "Well as much as I would love to go investigate, I don't think we can go there right now. It was pretty far. I mean I could fly, but I have no idea how to take you there with me."

"By any chance could Atsa take us out there? He seems to want to help and be knowledgeable about local areas," Amy replied.

"What a great idea! Maybe he can take us there tomorrow morning? It might be too dark and I was supposed to go visit my grandfather again tonight." I exclaimed.

Amy said seriously, "Well I imagine it would be too dark to see much of anything at night, plus even though I am not scared of you being a shapeshifter I wonder what all is lurking around in darkness. I would rather not find out especially if there is a spirit lurking about."

"Tomorrow it is. Here let's see if we can find out anything from mom's journal," I said.

We huddled up in a shaded corner leaning back against the freshly dug earth. The gritty dirt was digging into my legs, so I turned to sit on my bottom trying to get in a comfortable reading position. The pit was not so deep that the sunlight did not reach the bottom, so we could still see. The earth walls towered several feet over our heads and we were almost cool in the shade. Dusting off the diary, I looked around making sure there were no scorpions around us. I could feel a few newly freed worms wiggling behind my back, but I had grown accustomed to some creepy crawlies.

"I feel like we are in a tomb," murmured Amy as she looked up the steep walls of reddish dirt, "You really have been digging away. If archaeology doesn't work out, you could be a gravedigger."

7-27-93

Not finding those responsible has been weighing heavily on me. I have been ill for the last several weeks. Unfortunately, I have not been able to go out and help find those responsible and Clay has been keeping very busy trying to take care of me. He talked to my father as well. They have been trying to understand how my shapeshifting ability ties in with my sickness.

8-28-93

I discovered the reason for my sickness. I am to have a baby girl. She is due in just a few months. I am so excited to meet her. Now that I have been feeling better, I am preparing for her arrival. Clay wants to name her Kai which I think is fitting. I wonder if I will pass on my shapeshifting ability to her.

After reading this, Amy gave me a sharp look. I assumed that she wanted some more information on shapeshifting. One night I would show her. I'm sure it was both frightening and exciting for her to think about, much like it was for me the first time I discovered I could do this. I told her that I would show her later if she wanted. Seeing her nod, we went back to reading.

9-20-93

I was rifling through father's things yesterday and found some letters from a pipeline. They were interested in drilling some test wells around. I confronted my father about it and he said that the tribe would discuss it. However, since there was no compensation he thought that the tribe would be against it. I found it odd because the oil company had the same last name as Nikkoli. I thought he was trying to search for water.

12-12-93

I've just gotten back from the hospital with my new daughter. We were quite worried as she came early. Clay and father won't let me do much since the birth was so difficult. However, we are all home and resting. I can't wait to take her out on the dig site next year.

While reading through her diary, I couldn't help but get a little emotional. A tear trickled down my cheek as I thought about how much my mother must have loved me, yet I didn't even remember her. I made a vow to discover what had happened to her and my father and make those pay. Anger replaced my sadness as I wiped the tear away and continued reading.

2-22-94

It's been very busy with a newborn, but she is so happy and healthy. I can already see that she will be able to shapeshift into a falcon like me. Sometimes while she is sleeping her little toes curl up into claws. One day I will be able to show her how to do it and we can fly together.

I almost forgot even though the elders shut down the dig site months ago, there has been some activity. I also received a letter telling me to stop looking into oil and archaeology dig site connection. This came shortly after I had written a letter to Congress and the Governor about my suspicions about Petrov Petroleum Pipelines or P.P.P. Even though the letter had no return address or name, I knew it came from Nikkoli. It had his handwriting, plus he used my middle name. No one knew that.

3-12-94

I have been gathering evidence that Nikkoli was the one guilty of the thefts and threats. Today I wrote a letter exposing his secrets. I left a copy buried in my secret hiding spot in the cave and sent him a copy.

Clay discovered what I had done and he was very angry with me. He said, "You should just drop it, we have to take care of our daughter. Think of her protection!" He doesn't realize that I am protecting her. I am protecting her heritage. Not only her heritage, but even her shapeshifting ability is tied to this land. If something were to happen to destroy this dig site, it could possibly endanger both of our lives. According to legend if the valley of the falcon is destroyed then all who have descended from them will perish as well.

Once Clay understood that our lives hung on the survival of this valley and I wasn't just being stubborn he quickly joined in helping me formulate a plan to stop any drilling. We were going to punish those who messed up the dig site before as well.

4-1-94

This may be my last entry ever. If you are reading this then that means that you have discovered this journal where I buried it in my favorite hiding spot. It probably also means that I have been murdered so please make sure that this gets to my daughter one day.

I was sent a letter to meet at the dig site. While I am suspicious of this letter it my only hope that this meeting will result in the preservation of this site. I'm leaving my daughter in care of my father. Clay found out and would not hear of me confronting Nikkoli on my own. The letter and evidence ....

The clanking and rumbling of an engine coming to life interrupted our reading. We looked at each other, then up at the sky. Seeing that the sun had shifted in the sky, we knew that it was late afternoon. Amy's light eyes widened in surprise and horror, "Is that the van?"

I leapt to my feet and tried scrambling out of the hole quickly but couldn't quite reach the top. I tried again by taking a running start at the opposite end of the pit. Yet, I only managed to get a handful of dirt as my feet slid back down the wall unable to make it out. By now I was smudged with filth looking like a mud monster. I motioned my hand to Amy. "Here put your foot in my hand, I will boost you up! If you can get out, chase down the van and have someone come help me out too!"

Cupping my hands by clasping my fingers together, I watched as Amy placed her muddy boot on my palm. I used all my strength to heave her skinny frame up. Feeling my muscles straining I hoped that she made it on the first try. I felt her foot leave my hand and saw her pull herself up digging her elbows into the ground. Scrambling up her feet soon disappeared from view as well. Now I was just stuck down here by myself hoping that I wouldn't be stuck forever.

Her footsteps echoed on the hard ground carrying her further away from me and the dig site. I heard her calling out towards the bus and was imagining her frantically waving her arms. If nothing else if they were able to get Amy, then I could just fly safely away. That might take some explaining, but I am sure that Atsa could cover for me to keep my secret safe from the others.

Chapter 22

"That will teach them to be sticking their nose in where it doesn't belong", I thought as the van pulled away. The more Kai kept being stubborn and ignoring my advice to steer clear, the more I stopped caring about protecting Kai from my uncle. If she wouldn't listen and kept insisting on sticking around, I knew she wouldn't believe me later. My dreams of saving her were quickly fading.

Perhaps a night out in the desert would solve the dilemma for me. I'm sure the wolves or the spirits would get rid of the two of them. It would be hard for the authorities to *ignore the evidence if they were both dead and had the artifacts. It would look like their buyer had turned on them.*

If they managed to survive the night, perhaps they might actually be scared stiff. Especially if the little recording I had set up worked correctly. A haunted grave site might even scare them to death!

Slumping down in the dirt pit, I resigned myself to spending a long night out under the stars. That's when I heard footsteps pounding closer. Instead of calling out or trying to peer out, I made myself small in the corner trying to hide. For some reason I figured the footsteps were not a rescuer, but someone coming to finish me off just like they had my mother. Heck, it would be easy for them to just cover me up with dirt and no one would even know! Perhaps, I should try to find a makeshift weapon and fight off the assailant? The buzzing in my ears overshadowed all other sounds making me feel like I was inside a giant storm.

"Kai! The van already left and was out of sight by the time I got to the road," Amy panted sounding very out of breath.

My pounding heart slowed a bit when I realized that Amy had come back and I was not alone with a psychotic killer. Gradually, the world seemed to shift back to normal now that I was not panicking. However, a newfound fear set in when I realized we were both stuck out here without food or water and probably would be overnight. Amy couldn't just shapeshift and fly off like I could and I didn't really want to leave her here. We had some decisions to make and it didn't look like either were going to be pleasant.

"Great! Now what do we do? I'd say walk back, but it's a twenty-minute drive so that has to be at least fifteen miles. I don't think we are quite prepared to walk that distance," I whined. Kicking the dirt with the toe of my shoe.

Amy looked down on me as I paced the dirt chamber. I was contemplating how to get out of this mess. As of right now I was still stuck in the hole. "Well first of all do we want to be out in the open or do we want to hide in the excavation site? There aren't any trees out here to climb or to provide enough shade," Amy replied looking equally perplexed, "Let me see if I can find a ladder or bucket so you can climb out a bit easier." I saw her walk off towards where we left some equipment hoping that they hadn't loaded up everything.

I called out, "I wonder why they left so quickly? Do you think they left us on purpose?"

"Of course not! Why on Earth would they do that? I don't think we have a group of assassins impersonating archaeologists. They probably just forgot us and will be back shortly once they realize they left us," Amy replied calmly.

"If they notice..." I mumbled annoyed.

Amy came back over dragging a small three step ladder behind her. At least now I could get myself out. Her dirty clothes blended into the surrounding desert and while I had made fun of her dorky hat, but she seemed to be faring better out in the sun than I was. I decided to take part of my shirt and fashion it into a bandana to reflect the sun off of my head.

Clank clank clank. The ladder rattled when she dropped it by the edge of the hole and started to hand it down to me. Once it was in, I set it up and began to climb out. "What do you think we should do? I can fly back and alert the others, but I don't really want to leave you out here alone," I said.

"Let's just wait. I'm sure they will be back. We can try to figure out what your mother's journal means," Amy replied.

She was much more patient than I was, but I agreed that it would be a good idea to try to solve this together. After all, two heads were better than one. "Perhaps the letters will have some information. Too bad we can't just go there now. I wonder if there is any connection to the current oil company?" I asked.

"Hmm well if I remember correctly, I've seen signs with PPP on them. Perhaps that is the same company. We should probably research them a bit more. I wonder if they have any connections to anyone at the dig site?" Amy wondered.

"You mean the Elders?" I asked almost outraged hoping they were not in on this.

Amy shook her head, "No, I mean anyone on the dig. Do you think any of the interns have a connection?"

"It would be the perfect cover for them would it not?" I said.

"Didn't you also say that you were being watched in D.C.? There was a heist there and artifacts stolen here. Hardly seems like a coincidence especially since both seem to be inside jobs," Amy puzzled together.

"That makes sense! I suspected it was probably somebody on the dig since there was no way someone else would leave those notes to me in the va…" I trailed off.

ARH WOOOOO! ARH WOOO! The sound interrupted my reply. Amy's eyes grew large with fright. My head whipped around trying to decipher what the sound was and where it was coming from. The eerie sound started again and Amy grabbed my arm and pushed me into the pit right as she leapt in with me. "Hey what are you doing?" my muffled gasp came out.

"Shhhh" she whispered.

At this point I wasn't sure if I was more frightened of Amy or that strange sound. Maybe it had been her all along! Wouldn't that be crazy. I pushed out from underneath her and hit her over the head with the ladder knocking her out. As I looked at her lying there softly breathing I thought, "Now what?" I debated about leaving her here, but instead just felt really guilty. She was just trying to save me, yet I let fear overcome me and look where it had gotten me.

I walked over to shake her, but she wasn't waking up. The whole time the howling continued and I began speculate if the dig site was really cursed. At the moment it was adding up to be that way. I squeezed myself in the corner to hide and tried to think up a solution.

I saw Amy's eyes flutter open as her breath came out in a groan. She rubbed her head and shot me an accusatory look, "What was that about? I was just trying to keep you safe from the wolf."

"Well I feel sheepish. I'm sorry I reacted on an impulse. I thought you were attempting to silence me forever and were working with the killer," I stammered.

"Me?! You thought I was the killer? Seriously, Kai you need to work on your instincts. Why would I want to kill anyone? I'm boring and I rather like being boring. Usually that keeps me from getting bonked on the head, but you just had to drag me into your problems. I'm just trying to help you, not murder you. Although, now I sorta wish the latter were true. My head is going to hurt all night," she fumed her cheeks pink with anger.

I went over and gave her a hug hoping that would weaken her anger a bit and apologized. "Sorry, I freaked out and thought you were a killer. Thanks for trying to save me. I won't do it again. I've just been on edge with all this new stuff happening on top of all the threatening notes. It's like the world and me has gone crazy."

"I forgive you, but please talk quieter. I'm seriously scared to death of wolves and don't want those things coming over here. Do you want to be a meal for them?" Amy said.

We sat in silence for a moment trying to ignore the sounds as they got closer and closer until at least they seemed to disappear in the opposite direction. Once we couldn't hear them anymore Amy let out a sigh of relief. "I don't want to go back out there. What if they come back? Being ripped to shreds is not on my list of things to happen to me today. And don't even think about flying off and leaving me here like a bag of living Purina," Amy stated sternly.

"Did you have a bad experience with dogs or something? I mean I don't want to be eaten either, but I think they are more afraid of us than we are of them," I replied, "Relax, I won't leave you. If you have any ideas on how to get out of this debacle, then let me know."

Amy shivered, "You don't want to know," as she showed me the scars on her ankle, "let's just say I don't like sharp teeth and don't trust canines. My best bet it to wait til someone shows up. What's the worst that could happen?"

Chapter 23

The sound of footsteps and rattling boot spurs interrupted our conversation. The stomping seemed to get louder, then we heard a voice say, "I knew it was you all along."

A twangy voice replied, "Yes, but now you will be the last person to know. Your bones will forever haunt this Earth."

Bang, bang! A loud crack of a pistol split the air around us and the sound echoed off into the distance.

My head spun around and my shocked face met Amy's wide terrified eyes and I watched the blood drain from her face. I mouthed to her, "Ghosts or real?" She shrugged her shoulders but indicated that either option was horrifying. Honestly, I couldn't disagree with her on this one. First it was being left, then wolves, now some crazy ghosts or murderers. Considering that we never heard the second man's stringy high voice again it was safe to say that he was shot.

Stomp, rattle, stomp, rattle. The sounds got louder and louder seeming closer when all of a sudden it stopped. At this point we both scrunched up like a beetle rolling up into a ball in the corner hoping that whoever was coming closer would not see us. Either way my eyes were squeezed so tight, I could not see anything but little dots behind my eyelids.

Screech! The sound of a hawk caused me to peep an eye open. Its echo seemed familiar to me. Was that Atsa? Did he somehow sense that I was in danger? With one eye open I spotted sunlight glinted off a dark wing. Once I saw the distinct white tail feathers I knew it was Atsa. Feeling torn I wanted to both warn him away yet have him swoop in to save the day.

He circled above us in the dusk sky. The black outline of his form standing out against the blood red of the desert setting sun. I sat up and waved lightly up so he would know that we were down here. Before Amy could tackle me, I whispered, "That's Atsa. Looks like we won't be stuck here after all!" She looked skeptical at first, but when he glided down to land gracefully beside us in the pit Amy appeared more convinced.

Looking down at Atsa her face lit up with delight as she watched him begin his transformation from falcon to man. I noticed how amazed she was by the time she had to look up at him. "Wow! That is amazing! Can you do that again? What about you, Kai, can you both do that tranformer thing?"

"We aren't a sideshow," I said with a frown, "Did you see any ghosts or gunslingers while you were circling up above?"

Atsa looked at us both like we were mad, "If you mean the tumbleweeds? Then, yes, I saw those. That's the only thing out there."

"Just minutes ago, we heard someone get shot," Amy argued, "We might have imagined the wolves howling, but I am pretty sure we haven't gone desert mad and are hearing gunshots."

"First, let's get you guys out of here and we will take a look around," Atsa said.

Amy made a waving motion indicating that Atsa should go first. After he climbed up the rickety ladder, I followed putting one foot above the other. With each step I could feel the feet of the ladder push further into the sand making it seem like I was not climbing anywhere fast. Atsa reached down a hand and pulled me up the last little bit, then I turned to try to coax Amy out of the pit. Judging by the stubborn look on her face I had my work cut out for me.

Atsa called out, "Hey guys was this what you heard earlier?"

A second later we heard the boots and the gunshot which made both of us jump. He walked over closer holding a CD player and held his finger over the button to replay it again. "I think someone left this here to scare you," he announced, "When I didn't see you guys come back from the dig, I had assumed that you might have just forgotten to get on. The evidence seems to show that someone wanted you to miss van on purpose. Any ideas on who that might be?"

Amy nodded to me and we began to fill Atsa in on what we had learned in my mother's journal. He seemed as stunned as we were that we had stumbled upon a bit of a conspiracy. After a moment of pondering his face looked a bit more determined, "Let's reveal this monster and put him behind bars where he belongs," Atsa said fiercely.

"Are you going to help us?" I asked.

"Of course! You can't tell me a story like that and think I will just shrug my shoulders and walk away. First, I want to help you make peace with your past and also, I don't want this monster terrorizing our people. The mystery surrounding your mother and father's disappearance has long haunted our community and even convinced some that we should just sell the cursed land to the oil company to let them be cursed. However, I don't want to just hand over our heritage to thieving murderous criminals. It's also a great adventure," he added with a wicked grin that stole a piece of my heart.

I blushed as I smiled back, "I'm glad."

Amy rolled her eyes, "Alright now that we have that figured out, could we please figure out step one of the plan?"

"Step one? So anxious," Atsa replied.

She put her hand on her hip then waved to the surrounding area, "In case you didn't realize it we are stuck in the middle of the desert. It's really hard to catch a criminal stranded out here. How are we going to get back? Maybe you guys can just fly back, but I can't."

"She's right. We are stuck out here. Luckily not with ghosts, but either way we can't warn the others, try to find more information, nor find this villain," I muttered as I paced back and forth.

Right about then a cloud of dust appeared surrounding a Jeep that roared to a stop. Red hot sparks flew from the rusty muffler spraying the darkness like a sparkler on the 4th of July. The door swung open and out popped a figure that was hard to see in the dusk, but slowly the features materialized shadows and I saw it was Johanna. Then I saw Ahiga's familiar face through the driver's side window. "What?

You don't think I would fly out here without backup, do you?" Atsa chuckled, "As soon as the van came back without you both, I knew something was wrong. I had decided to fly out here in case you needed quicker assistance and had told your cousin to follow with the Jeep."

Now that we could all get back safely, we filled the whole group in on the plan. I could tell that it pained my grandfather to hear the details of my mother's journal just as it had made me feel bitter as well. While I hadn't known my mother, I was very angry that someone had taken her away that opportunity.

"I think your original idea is the best. The answer lies with that document that your mother buried. You will go there tomorrow instead of to the dig site. I will explain how this is also important to the tribe and possibly even the current thefts," Ahiga explained, "Nothing would please me more than to see these sociopaths to their own grave."

Amy shook her head in puzzlement, "What I don't understand is why did this start up again? There were thefts before, then it stopped after your mom went missing, and now it's happening again. The dig site has been open for several years now, you'd think they would have finished what they started before now."

"The reason is that Congress is going to vote to pass the pipeline to go through our lands unless we find something substantial to prove that this area is holy and important to our people. Even though, we were able to circumvent the issue for years it is out of our control now. Especially, since several of the Congressmen own stock in the pipeline that is going through our lands," Ahiga sighed heavily, "It doesn't matter that I along with others have served this country and were able to use our language to prevent our enemies during World War II from understanding our troop movement. They are just greedy and want everything for themselves."

I drew my brows together into an M and grumbled, "That's so unfair! Why are they allowed to do that?"

"Because they make their own rules," Atsa grumbled, "Don't get me wrong there are some good politicians hopefully, but most are just looking after themselves. It's our duty to vote out the corruption and greed or we can stop it in its track right here on the reservation. By finding the connection between this Nikkoli guy with the pipeline, senators, and his involvement in both your parents' disappearance and artifact theft we can stop the pipeline. Perhaps, even some will be convicted if they can prove their involvement."

Feeling somehow more empowered I nodded and couldn't wait to see what we would discover the next day. In the darkness I smiled at the group and said, "Tomorrow at dawn we will meet up and I will take you guys to the cave. Since I only know how to get to it from the air, Atsa and I will fly there, and you guys can follow by the ground. Who's in?"

A chorus of "I am" echoed in the twilight followed by a deep grumble, "I will stay back for I fear I will hold you up. However, I will keep track of time and send the authorities when they are needed," Ahiga added.

Thus it was settled that the four of us would go by air and land tomorrow to solve this decades old crime that had deeply affected my entire life. Now that we had a plan, we decided to head back before it got any later.

Chapter 24

After a short sojourn through the dark desert under the clearest starlight sky I had yet to witness we arrived back at the campsite. I was quite thankful to be safe and have food and water. This night could have turned out entirely different. What was even worse was that we found out that it wasn't by accident that the van left, someone had told them we had already went back to camp. That someone wanted an alternative ending for tonight, one where did not come back alive. Just thinking about it made my skin crawl. They wouldn't be so bold as to try something, tonight would they? Feeling the blood drain from my face and my fingers turn to icicles, I couldn't help the foreboding sense that something bad was going to happen. A cold sweat broke out on my brow and I felt faint collapsing onto the hard ground.

"Kai, Kai" I heard my name being whispered as I was being shook and I looked up into Atsa's concerned chocolate eyes and almost melted into them. "Are you okay?"

"I'm fine, but I don't want to stay in the camp tonight. I can't shake the feeling that if I do stay here, it will be my last night," I stammered.

"Once we get some food, I will take you somewhere safe okay?" Atsa reassured me.

I nodded as he helped me to my feet. We walked into the tent to get some dinner before it was too late. That's when I noticed something odd, there were a few women and men walking purposefully through camp wearing FBI t-shirts. It must be serious if the FBI was being called in to investigate an archaeologist heist.

I can't believe that they didn't find those artifacts that I hid in Kai's jacket and her tent! Are these investigators buffoons? I practically showed them where to look and even kept Kai away so she couldn't find them herself. The locals couldn't handle it and had to call in the FBI. I had seen a Detective Nataliya and some young man walking around camp taking notes. I made a point of befriending them and trying to lead them to think Kai was the culprit, but they didn't seem to find my advice worth any merit. Not only did they not listen, but they seemed to not be looking for the artifacts at all. The young man was just walking around holding various objects. It was a bit bizarre.

Apparently, I was cunning enough that I wasn't a suspect, but not adept enough to frame Kai successfully. Inwardly, I fumed like a runaway train because my plans had not worked out. Especially now that I saw both Kai and her friend were rescued from the desert. They weren't even stuck out there a night. Neither of them seemed too worse for wear, no broken bones, cuts, or bruises. Abandoning them out there had been risky because the lie could be traced back to me. I had told the others that Atsa had come and picked them up earlier. The liability was immense considering that they were only out there for a few hours and had survived completely intact!

Edging closer to the investigators I overheard, "We didn't find any artifacts nor signs of foul play. However, I do feel like there is more going on here than meets the eye. For some reason someone wants us to think it's a crew member. Yet, I felt something more sinister. We need to call in reinforcements."

They were getting too close. Leaving the girls at the dig site had not been enough. I needed to end this before my role was discovered. Ducking behind some tents and scrub brush I got out my phone and texted my uncle.

Me: [The girls will be at the cave tomorrow afternoon. They found the proof. Bring back up. I will follow them there and leave them with you.]

The cold food tasted delicious to our growling stomachs and we scarfed the food down so quickly we didn't even need silverware. I was licking my sticky fingers when the FBI wandered over in our direction. I glanced at Atsa wondering if we should tell them what we knew, but I saw him shake his head. He apparently was not that trustful of the government and I supposed growing up on the reservation had something to do with that. Plus, you never knew who was profiting from this pipeline. I saw the advantages of feeling out the agents before involving them in our own problem. They could detain us if we weren't careful or perhaps even ruin our own private investigation that we were going to do tomorrow. It was best to wait until we had the evidence in our hands and perhaps even a photograph copy just in case it fell into the wrong hands.

Officer Nataliya spoke first, "Hello. I'm leading the investigation into the missing artifacts both here and in Washington D.C. If you have any information or leads that would be helpful. Have you seen anyone suspicious around there lately?"

"No," I lied, "Everything seemed normal, well normal for an exciting summer working at a field school, but nothing seemed out of the ordinary until we heard some artifacts went missing. I hope you guys catch whoever is responsible."

"We do too. Unfortunately, there is not a lot of evidence and everyone here seems rather tight lipped. If you know anything please don't hesitate to call or text," a young man said as he handed me his card. Our hands brushed as I took it, "My name is Ezra by the way. I help my mom in some cases. I have a special sense as you could call it." He smiled ruefully at us. For some reason he looked familiar like I had seen him on the news or something. I made a mental note to look him up later.

"Thank-you. I will let you know, but us interns rarely know anything useful or so they tell me," I laughed trying to make light of the situation.

I saw Ezra exchange a knowing look with his mother and thought we were toast. Nevertheless, neither one seemed to want to call us out on our lie and they said their goodbyes. I wished them luck on their search and we all tried to escape the tent without drawing attention to ourselves. As we were leaving Amy said, "You know I saw Alex leaving our tent the other day and I wonder if he left anything incriminating in there?"

"What makes you think that he wants to frame me?" I asked truly concerned.

Amy shrugged, "I'm not sure exactly. He just had a weird vibe about him is all. It just struck me as a bit odd that he would be in our tent. You didn't send him there or ask him to meet you did you?"

I frowned, "No, I did not. That is odd. Perhaps I should go check things out."

Trying not to frantically race, we walked with purpose to the tent where we found it already thoroughly ransacked by the FBI. I didn't see any artifacts laying around and luckily, I had my mother's journal tucked discreetly into my bag. Therefore, I didn't think that they had any evidence against me.

Amy said, "I don't feel comfortable sleeping here. Can we go somewhere else?"

"I had said the same thing to Atsa earlier. He has somewhere in mind. Let's grab what we will need for tonight and for tomorrow and follow him," I replied.

I stuffed some of my scattered clothes in my bag along with some toiletries and headed off. We followed Atsa who was using his phone flashlight to navigate to my cousin's jeep. He waited until we were inside and buckled in to divulge where we would be spending the night. "Sorry, I didn't mean to keep you in suspense, but if we are worried about someone in the camp we probably shouldn't tell them where we are going right? Anyways I think that the best option is to go stay at your Grandfather's house since we already want to leave from there in the morning. Plus, Ahiga has some awesome stories to tell about his days as a code talker!"

"That sounds great! Are you going to stay there too? I'd feel safer knowing you were there," I murmured.

"Why Kai are you worried about me? Who knew that you cared about my safety so much?!" Atsa slyly said.

"Hmmp. More like I am just worried that if you go missing it will just be easier to kill us off that's all. Plus, you are helping us,

I'd hate to lose someone on our side of this war. Hopefully, you can take care of yourself though," I replied in a teasing tone. Looking back at Amy I saw her roll her eyes.

Atsa had his head turned back laughing we heard a loud thunk hit the windshield. Jumping in our seats I barely held in a scream as we looked around the darkness to see what had hit us. Through the moonlight we didn't see anything around us and the windshield had not broken. So, we carefully continued on, but were reminded that these were perilous times. We rode the rest of the way in a blanket of silence.

All the lights were strangely off at Ahiga's house which put me on edge. Did he not know that we were coming to visit? Amy looked at me and I shrugged, then we heard the door creak open as my grandfather stepped out. Quietly, he motioned through the darkness for us to come in. Amy followed skeptically probably assuming that we were leading her to her death. I sincerely hoped that I would not be doing that tomorrow. I knew that we were going to be safe for the night.

Once we were safely inside, Atsa hid the Jeep behind the barn so if anyone were to drive by they would not think Ahiga had visitors. He was taking a lot of time to ensure that no one had followed us, which in retrospect made me realize the gravity of the situation we were facing. We weren't just some kids who stumbled upon a prank or a simple thief. This was serious business that could get us killed.

Ahiga greeted us with hand modeled clay cups brimming with kettle steeped tea. The smell of chamomile drifted softly into my nostrils. Taking the cup from his hand I sat cross legged on the well-worn woven rug in the middle of the living room. I ran my fingertips over the pattern trying to trace the hawk that was in the middle.

Within a few minutes Ahiga's gentle voice started with an even tone as he reminisced over his years past. He told us when he was just a little older than we were that he was recruited to be a code talker during World War II. He said, "At first going to boot camp and being the top in my class since I grew up knowing how to survive was exciting. I made several friends with whom I thought I'd be lifelong friends. Yet, very quickly we discovered that war was not the glory we were seeking. Once we made it to the front lines in the Pacific, it wasn't all palm trees and blue seas. It quickly became a sea of death. Yet, we endured and never was our code broken. So even at a young age, we were able to make a contribution that saved the world. Much like the achievements your mother made in so short of time and what you all will accomplish tomorrow."

A small smile pulled at my lips as I rose to give Ahiga a hug. "Thanks for sharing, it's definitely inspirational for tomorrow. I can't believe I have so many stories to catch up on, I will have to come back more frequently to hear them all," I murmured in his ear trying to keep my emotions in check. I saw his eyes well up and I couldn't stop my own tears then. I had missed so much about my grandfather and parents since this Nikkoli guy had taken them from me. I really hope that creep got what was coming to him, otherwise I feared I would devote my life to ruining his. As much as I loved my aunt and uncle who I thought of as my parents, I really wished I would've been given the opportunity to get to know a part of myself I didn't realize was missing until now.
"I know my child," he whispered, "I wish you could've known your mother. But I do know that she would be so proud of you. Tomorrow you will find justice for her, I can feel it in my old bones."

With that I excused myself and made my way to a guest room to drift off to dreamland.

Chapter 25

Psst! A whisper woke me up from a deep slumber where I had been dreaming of soaring the skies with my mother. I felt myself falling through the clouds until I landed with a thump on the bed. Groggily, I blinked my blurry eyes open and meet a pair of shiny dark eyes. Turning red at realizing Atsa was in my room I stammered, "What are you doing?"

"You dreaming of flying?" he asked smiling.

Bewildered I nodded, "Yes, how did you guess? You still didn't answer why you are creeping on me sleeping." I narrowed eyes looking down my nose at him.

He reached up and pulled a tawny feather from my hair and said, "I was told to wake you up. It's time to start today's adventure. Are you ready?"

"As ready as I will ever be. Let's find a way to lock up this psycho for life," I confirmed as I rolled out of bed. Hoping that there was enough food for breakfast, I followed Atsa into the kitchen where Amy, Johanna, and Ahiga were eating some toast and eggs.

"About time you woke up! We thought maybe you snuck out and went there early. Or that you flew off," Ahiga said with a laugh.

Amy looked puzzled and asked, "So you know Kai can turn into a hawk and so can Atsa. Can all of you do this? I'm a little confused. I just wanna know what we are dealing with today. Otherwise, it seems like I am the only one holding you all back since I can't fly. Unless it's in the water around here, then maybe I can."

"It's not in the water. There's a special genetic ability that is passed down. The legend claims that the ability started when someone murdered a family member. It's sort of gruesome, but several people have the ability yet have not done anything evil. Although, it is said that we will constantly have to battle evil in our lives to make up for what our ancestor did do. However, I am just glad that we aren't evil. Just like there are good and bad vampires I suppose, there are good and bad Skin walkers. This is not the first time I have had to use my ability to fight off the bad, but I have a feeling that was just a test for the real thing. Ahiga over here used his ability to gather information during the war and help defeat the Axis powers," Atsa explained.

"Now it's your turn," Ahiga smiled at me.

I picked up a crispy piece of bacon and savored the taste before I replied sarcastically, "No pressure or anything."

Finishing up my plate, I licked the grease off my fingers before buttering my toast and stuffing it in my mouth. We wanted to get an early start, and since I saw the sun starting to peek through the windows, it was time to go. I gave my backpack to Amy to take in the Jeep while Atsa and I got ready for our flight.

Watching Johanna and Amy get in the Jeep, I took a deep breath and tried to envision myself soaring in the clouds. Before I knew my arms started moving on their own accord and flapping lifting me higher and higher. I looked down with the wind ruffling my feathers and saw Atsa smiling up at me as he started to flap his arms. Once his transformation was complete he joined and we soared into the clouds playing a game of tag before dipping down far enough to be seen by the girls on the ground. I did not want to fly too high or fast and lose them. Stretching my wings wide, I sort of floated on the breeze slowly dipping my wings one way then the other to ride the air stream. With Atsa by my side it felt almost peaceful and serene flying above the Earth and I wished we could do this again sometime when my life wasn't in danger. It was so peaceful that I had almost forgotten that part.

Peering below I saw the dust being kicked up by the Jeep's tires and was glad that they were able to follow the best they could without any real roads. Luckily, this area was flatter with hard sand and not full of rocky outcrops so they wouldn't fall into a ditch. There weren't many thick shrubs or cacti either so this area must get some traffic if it wasn't overgrown. While I was looking down I felt something whoosh by my face and scanned the sky for Atsa thinking he was playing with me, but instead I saw a huge bird flying right towards him. I shrieked in warning and he dipped out of the way. I had never thought of being in danger as prey.

By chance a rabbit hopped out from some brush below which distracted the bird as it dove for a much easier dinner. My heart was hammering in my chest by the time Atsa drifted over to me and I realized that being a hawk did not mean we were at the top of the food chain. Fortunately, we weren't far from the cave and I could see the hill outcrop not far in the distance. If we could make it there without being attacked by a larger bird of prey we would be in the clear. Flapping harder to go faster I flew with a purpose now. The cave opening got closer and closer. I had stopped caring if the Jeep was right behind us or not, I just wanted to be safe.

My claws reached out and clasped a rocky ledge near the cave opening. Upon landing I quickly shook my head and envisioned myself human again. Feeling my feathers disappear I opened my eyes to see my hands transform and grow from wingtips to fingers. Even my blue nail polish showed through the feathers as my fingers returned to normal. Within a blink I was human again and safe from hungry eagles. Phew!

Minutes later Atsa landed and made his transformation. "Whoa! That was pretty close and cool huh?"

"Cool? We almost got eaten! You're crazy!" I exploded.

I knew that they were going to look for the documents today. I had already told my uncle and he should already be in position. I just had to follow them and make sure there were no surprises. I didn't really trust Uncle Nikkoli to hold up his end of the agreement. He had always been a cad able to slip out of situations with the ease of a jackal. In addition to, he literally was getting away with murder. Well he wasn't going to get away with killing either my sister or myself.

I had followed the dust that the Jeep had stirred up and hoped that they couldn't see me. When we reached the rocky cliffs, I saw Kai and Atsa clambering up the crumbly hillside. Wiping the sweat from my brow with my bandana I prepared for the grudging climb ahead. I couldn't wait to be done with all of this nonsense and have it be over.

Behind Atsa I heard the sound of gravel falling and figured our landing stirred loose some pebbles. I turned to start looking for where the journal had been to find the additional documents that my mother had hidden. That's when I heard a distinct cock of a gun much like you'd hear in a Western movie. I froze with one foot in the air, then swung around to see where the sound had come from.

That's when I came face to face with a very cranky middle-aged man. He was wearing a fancy suit, but it was the sun glinting off the silver pistol barrel that really drew my attention. Why was this guy here and wearing a suit? That had to be uncomfortable in the desert. Perhaps we were trespassing on his land and he was on his way to church or a funeral? That's when I heard Atsa say, "Hey we don't want any trouble here. Just put the gun down and we can talk."

"I don't think we will be doing any talking. I want your friend here to take me to the documents," he said with a strong Russian accent. His icy blue eyes met mine and I saw desperation and hate ooze out like a plague.

For some reason he didn't look like he was just upset that we were walking on his sand. Before I could say anything Atsa moved in front me, blocking the man from grabbing me. Without hesitation he shot Atsa. I screamed as I heard the bullet explode and hit him in the shoulder. His whole body jerked before he collapsed in front of me. Oh my God! What had I done? I drug him into this and now because of me he would die out here in the middle of nowhere and I would join him shortly I was sure.

I had to think fast. I pushed that anguish down inside of me to focus on what had to be done. If I wanted to save myself and perhaps have a chance of rescuing Atsa before he bleed to death I needed to on top of my game. "Where are the documents?" asked the creepy Russian voice.

Without hesitation I said, "They are down this way in the cave. Follow me. I still have to find them. I think they are under a rock shaped like a lizard."

His pale white face looked back to where I had pointed in the cave. With him distracted I used my toe to cover up the hole where I had found my mother's journal and I bolted back down the path. With a flying leap I jumped into the air hoping that I was able to transform before I hit the ground. Moving my arms, I felt myself gain lift and I rose into the sky. I heard a loud curse, then the sound of bullets being fired. They echoed off of the rock walls around me and one struck me in the wing. Flapping wildly, I tried to keep from falling, but it was too late. Tail spinning out of control I landed in a heap towards the bottom of the canyon.

Noticing my feathers disappearing I tried not to panic. Apparently, I couldn't shapeshift while injured and my arm was bleeding from where the bullet had grazed my wing. I heard him walking down the path and a torrent of gravel poured down indicating he was close by. I tried to hide under a rock, but I heard him shouting and swearing.

"You are just delaying the inevitable, I will find you. Come on out and I will make your death a quick one. Much quicker than your parents." His thick Russian accent made him difficult to understand. Did he just mention my parents? I perked up because my parents had long been dead.

"Yes, that's right. I know the truth about your parents, the truth that everyone has been keeping from you. If you come down, I will give you the answers that you seek," his accent getting thicker and his words seeming to drip honey.

Knowing I should not trust this brute, curiosity got the best of me and I sputtered involuntarily, "You knew my parents..?"

"I more than knew your parents, my dear. We were the best of friends until they betrayed me that is. For that they had to pay the price. I am Nikkoli Petrov," he said nonchalantly. Then he yelled, "Gotcha!" I heard the bullet travel down the gun chamber and through the air coming right in my direction. What seemed like hours passed while I stared frozenly at the bullet spinning towards my head. Unable to move out of the way in my trance, I felt a force slam into me and a piercing pain at my temple.

Feeling sluggish, I felt my mind fog over. I was drifting back in time, back to the beginning of the summer. The sound of maniacal laughter was the last thing I heard as my world went black. The only thing on my mind was this guy must be Nikkoli and he had killed my parents. The very man I had tried to put away was here and wanted me dead now.

Chapter 26

Groggily, I opened my eyes to see two wait no three men hovering over me, no there were only two now. Trying to focus I saw that there was only one man standing above me. His outline hazy against the sun, but I heard him laughing. He kicked my foot and placed his boot over the wound on my arm and said, "Tell me where the documents are and I will finish you quick. Otherwise, I will make your suffering last for days." The voice seemed to fade in and out making it hard to determine where it was coming from.

Blinking my eyes, I fought off the fog that was blanketing my mind. I needed to focus if I was going to get out of this alive. Lifting my hand, I put it on my pounding temple.

My fingers touched something sticky and I pulled my hand around to my face and saw they were covered scarlet blood. I had to fight off a wave of nausea, I had never been able to stand the sight of blood. Don't pass out, don't pass out I kept saying to myself. Finally, by controlling my breathing and focusing on something else I was able to calm my racing heart and adjust my eyes so they would focus.

Seeing the dark form above me, I looked carefully to see if he was armed hoping he lost his weapon somehow. Unfortunately, my luck had not improved while I was out like a light. He stood holding a very scary looking pistol and had another gun that looked more like a cannon. His facial expression was not one of sympathy as he looked down on me and I knew that if I gave him what he wanted he would just shot me again or leave me to slowly die. Which when you added up the blood loss, the heat already starting to rise, and lack of water I did not calculate my odds to be that great. Even if my cousin happened to find me hidden away in this crevice. I did not figure that another bullet would increase my odds of survival, so I tried to concoct a story to perhaps send him on a wild goose chase. It needed to be believable. Then, I screamed out in agony, "You'll never make me tell you!"

His boot came down hard on my wounded arm causing me to cry out in agony. "Okay! Okay! It's under the second rock by the entrance!"

His face turned into a wicked grimace and I was not sure if he believed me or not. "I will go check it out, it's not like you can get far," he said with an evil chuckle. "If my idiotic nephew would have finished you when he had the chance none of this would be necessary. He had it all set up to frame you for the missing artifacts. Alex said that he hid them in your tent, but he must have gotten scared. That little punk never could get anything right. I will take care of him after I am done with you, not to worry."

"Alex has been working for you this whole time?" I gasped out. I knew I should've just let him leave, but there was so much new information that I wanted to keep it straight. Especially, if Alex escaped or decided to come after me later.

"Pshh of course! You didn't think he was really that interested in you, did you? He doesn't know the first thing about archaeology, Alex just knows the value of artifacts on the black market. Which was useful for me. Yet, he managed to muck up my plans once again. You'd think he wasn't part of the family the way that he can't stomach disposing of a pesky little girl," he ranted.

I decided to keep quiet and let him go on his wild goose chase. He was certifiably insane. Not only had he killed my parents, he had enlisted his nephew to kill and frame me? What a nutcase! This psycho needed to behind bars asap. At least he needed me to find his papers so perhaps I could survive long enough to put him where he belonged.

As he turned to go back up the slope I noticed another figure up further on the cliff. He looked vaguely familiar, then his face came in more clearly. He must have seen the shocked look on my face because he held up a finger. It was Alex! Great! I thought, another person wanting my demise. Did he follow his uncle? Why was he hiding?

The next thing I saw was a boulder careening down a cliff headed straight towards Nikkoli. There was no time for him to leap out of the way. I heard him scream as the large rock slammed into him crushing him into the ground. The only thing that stuck out was his pale elongated fingers that twitched slightly. Nikkoli was about as harmful as the Wicked Witch of East now. More dirt avalanched down the path and I leaped out of the way to avoid any landing on me.

Walking closer I noticed that Nikkoli had stopped moving and there probably wasn't anything to be done to save him. Not that I really wanted to anyways. I saw the shadow of Alex above me and for a second worried that he would crush me to death as well. Instead of seeing a boulder fly at me, he just gave me a salute, then turned his back to return to wherever he had come from. I had a feeling that I would not see him again at the camp or dig site. Perhaps, not ever again. I figured as long as he left me alone, I wouldn't go chasing trouble that I didn't need. I had justice for my parents, I had the evidence to hand over to the FBI, and all would be well.

I heard footsteps shuffling up behind and I turned to see who it was prepared to hide, run, or fight depending on the situation. Relief washed over me seeing Johanna's familiar friendly face and smiling dark eyes. "Hey are you alright? We heard gunshots, screams, and oh my gosh! You are bleeding!" Johanna rambled worriedly. She rushed over to my side checking to see how bad my injuries were. "What happened?"

I pointed at Nikkoli's crushed body under the boulder and began to recount the events to her. She pulled me into a hug and assured me that everything would be okay. "Atsa is still up there, we need to get him to medical care quickly! I left the documents hidden and I need to grab those as well," I told her. Amy's head peaked out above some rocks. She looked sweaty and out of breath. Clearly not as used to the desert heat as Johanna was.

"What did I miss?" she panted with her hands on her knees.

I smiled and replied laughing shakily, "A lot! Sounds about right to show up right when everything has been solved."

Following each other like pack mules we began our ascend to the top of the cliff where the entrance to the cave was. I heard Amy stumble a few times behind me and looked to make sure she didn't fall. By this point I was completely covered in sweat and a thick coating of dust and I am sure that I looked a sight. My foot landed in some soft dry dirt and slid down some ways causing me to fall forwards. Luckily, I caught myself before I landed face first in a pile of rocks, but I did manage to bloody my hands with the fall.

At last I made it to the top, the exhaustion and blood loss was starting to set in. Filing over carefully so we didn't fall over the edge, I made it to Atsa. I shook his shoulder and he groaned as his eyes popped open scaring me half to death. "Atsa! Can you hear me? Do you think you can stand?"

"Where are the documents again?" Amy called over her shoulder as she was rolling rocks over here and there.

I pointed to where I had moved a rock over a hole and said, "Over there."

Atsa's voice cracked as he said, "I think I can stand, but everything hurts. Where is that madman?"

Hazel eyes met his deep dark eyes as I said, "He's dead. Alex showed up and pushed a boulder on him and ran off. I take it that he wanted him dead for his own purposes and wasn't changing sides."

His eyes skimmed over me and I felt my cheeks flush while awareness crept over me. The concern I saw in them made a lump appear in my throat. "You're bleeding," he whispered holding a hand up to carefully cup my face.

"It's just a scratch. It would've been much worse had you not stepped in front of his gun," I murmured.

"Alright you two. Stop making eyes at each other. Do you want to get out of here or not? I found the documents. From the looks of it both of you could use a hospital," Amy grumbled as she walked out of the cave papers in hand.

Both Johanna and Amy took each of us by the arm and let us lean on them as we hobbled back down towards the car. Neither Atsa or I were strong enough to make the transformation to fly back to town more quickly than the Jeep. Every step was painful and when we finally made it to the Jeep I let myself close my eyes and fall into a deep sleep. The Jeep jostling me as I lay propped up against Atsa.

As I ran down the rocky path, I didn't look back. I had no reason to do so. That was in the past and I was moving towards the future. A future in which I was free of my Uncle and his influence. I would start over somewhere with my sister. Judging by the look on Kai's face I wouldn't see her again, but that look also said she would not turn me in either. On a rocky desert mountain, we had reached a compromise of sorts.

I took care of both of our problems when I heaved the boulder down the cliff. I just couldn't take his insults and the control he held over me anymore. Also, I was beginning to doubt that he was going to let my sister and I live through this ordeal. I guess I had snapped, but let's be real the world was rid of just one more creep. Now I was free and my possibilities for the future were endless. Trudging my way back through the desert, I hoped to be able to catch a bus in town.

After several hours of walking my feet were dragging through the dusty gravel and I would kill for a drink of water when I saw the sign for the bus station come into view. Luckily, I had kept some of the money for fencing the artifacts instead of giving it to my Uncle. Going from shuffling to jogging I was panting by the time I made it to the ticket counter. I was covered in sienna colored dust which just made me blend in with the rest of the vagabonds waiting at the bus station. I asked for a water and paid for a ticket on a bus headed east.

After I made my purchases, I boarded the bus as night settled over the area like a blanket. I started to ponder the limitless options for future. Perhaps I would join the carnival with my sister. I hear they hire younger kids. Additionally, I have plenty of talents and I would be harder to find since we would be on the move constantly. Neither my uncle's cronies nor the cops would think to look there.

Chapter 26

Bright lights blinded me when I opened my eyes and the smell of bleach stung my nose. Judging by the white walls and the constant beeping sound in my ear, I was in a hospital. My mouth felt like I swallowed a cotton ball and my head both ached and felt like an ocean was sloshing around inside. I reached for a water bottle that was sitting next to my bed and drank the whole thing. That's when I realized I was not alone.

Atsa was in the bed beside mine, his eyes were shut, and he was as bandaged up as I was. Knock, knock! I heard a light rapping sound on the door before it opened. I was expecting Johanna or Grandfather, but instead three strangers came in all with FBI jackets on. I recognized two of them from the dig: a middle-aged woman and a younger man. However, I didn't recognize the wild haired girl. As they came closer I read their names badges and saw one was Officer Nataliya, Ezra, and Zoe. She looked just like my Instagram friend! I can't believe she showed up here. I was going to contact her, but I guess now I don't have to. What a coincidence!

Officer Nataliya began by introducing themselves and said, "We are part of a special investigative group within the FBI. We look into the more peculiar cases as some of us have special skills. We know that you have some abilities as well."

"What do you mean abilities?" I asked confused.

"Shape shifting," Ezra added quickly.

"Oh," I responded sounding a bit defeated. I was rather hoping that no one else would know.

"Don't worry we aren't here to put you in an X-men style prison, we just want to help solve this case," Officer Nataliya added.

"Trust me, I met them a few years ago and was just scared as you are. Yet as you can see they haven't performed weird experiments on me or killed me. They are pretty amazing at their jobs," Zoe smiled in my direction.

Officer Nataliya continued, "Anyways, after dropping you and Atsa off at the hospital your cousin came straight to me. We have the evidence that ties Nikkoli and his company to the artifact thefts from your parents' time. Now that we have that information we are building a case to connect him with the current issues at the site. A warrant was issued to search his business, phone, and home. We recovered his body and the company can't really exist without him, but we are doing our best to navigate through the red tape. As we find out more information we will of course share that with you."

Atsa woke up then and added, "Does this mean that the pipeline won't go through?"

"We are working on that. Some in Congress are still pushing, but once the murders come out to the public we believe that the pipeline will not go through and may possibly lead to more arrests. Several Congressmen are already being indicted as we speak for campaign funds coming from Petrov and there are some emails to suggest that they knew about his past yet choose to do business with him anyways," Officer Nataliya continued.

"Murders? What murders?" I croaked over the hoarseness of my throat.

Officer Nataliya looked confused then said, "Of your parents. You do know that they were murdered right?"

"I guessed, but I didn't think that we would be able to recover their bodies," I mumbled sadly.

"That's what we are here for. We are good at finding things even those that don't want to be. I have had some feelings out by the dig site, but we wanted to wait until you were released from the hospital. Then you would be able to go with us if you wanted," Zoe explained.

I wasn't sure how I felt about this. It would be nice to have closure and know that they did not just run off to Mexico. Deep down I knew they were dead and had even accepted that as a reality, but part of me did not want hard evidence to prove it to be true. That evidence would further prove Nikkoli's guilt and ensure that a pipeline would not go through. Which was what my mother would have wanted. After reading her journal I knew that she would not have wanted her death to be in vain and would even be at peace if it had helped the rest of the tribe.

Slowly I nodded and said, "Yes, I want to be there. When can you spring me from this prison?"

"The doctors claim that you can leave tomorrow. They want to keep you overnight and make sure you don't have any issues. Atsa, however, needs a few more days. The bullet was lodged in his shoulder requiring an operation to remove it," Officer Natalia replied, "We will be back tomorrow then. You get some rest."

I waved as they walked out and turned towards Atsa to see that he had been awake to hear the whole conversation. He looked as miserable as I felt. He croaked out, "Sorry about your parents. I wish I could've met them. They might be able to help me figure out why you are so amazing."

I couldn't help, but blush before I replied, "Thanks. You can meet my adoptive parents, I am sure that they helped form me into me too. It's good to know I still turned out alright even if my parents weren't alive to help raise me."

"I think your drive, passion, determination, and perhaps your stubbornness was inherited from your mom. You couldn't escape that gene," he smiled, "Which are the things I like the most about you. Perhaps, your adoptive parents could come out here sometime."

There was another soft rap at the door and it swung upon to reveal the only parents I had ever known along with Amy who lingered in the back! It was fairly ironic that they had shown up in that moment, but not odd that they knew I was in the hospital. Their faces were etched with worry. My mother's blue eyes were brimming with tears and her puffy red cheeks indicated that she had been crying for some time. My dad held a hand to the small of her back and gently pushed her inside. I couldn't believe how much I had missed them and was surprised that I hadn't even thought of them coming out here. I had just assumed that they thought I was safe at the camp. I felt my heart swell with joy and tried to sit up and run to them. I got all tangled in the wires and IV lines while trying to get up to go hug them. I winced at the pain in my shoulder and within seconds my mom was there hugging me and telling me to lay back. "We were so worried when we got the phone call from your Grandfather. This is why we never brought you back to this place. I also had a bad feeling about your parents' disappearance and thought something might happen to you too!" my mother wailed.

"Now you know it wasn't Ahiga, but the person who murdered Lina and Clay who is responsible. I heard from the FBI and your cousin that justice was served there and we now know what happened all those years ago. Kai is mostly alright and she will be alright now that we are here. I am sure when she comes back in the future things won't be quite as crazy, right Kai?" my dad told my mother and asked me as he gave me a pointed look.

I couldn't help but feel a little bad for worrying them both so much. I should have called or stayed out of danger, but I knew that I did the right thing by finding my mother's killer. I hoped that they would understand. I was rather shocked that my father mentioned me coming back and the look on my mom's face said she would take some convincing. "I can come back and visit Grandpa? I really want to hear more of his code talker stories. I promise I won't find any trouble next time. Nikkoli is dead and I don't see anyone else trying to stir up trouble around here," I pleaded.

"Don't worry. I will keep a close eye on her and keep her safe," Atsa coughed as he was still recovering from his chest wound.

My dad smiled and reached out a hand to shake Atsa's and said, "I want to thank you for trying your best now to keep my little girl safe. I still wished you guys would have let the cops handle it, but what's done is done."

Looking my mom in the eye I asked, "Mom will you stay with me tonight? I really don't want to stay here, but that might help if you were here."

"Of course! You know wild horses couldn't keep me away," she hugged me tight.

I winced, "Hey watch the bruises."

"Sorry!" she said as she pulled up a chair to sit next to me.

Amy and Johanna both entered then and I was relieved to see that they had made it unscathed. They both gave me a hug and apologized for not waiting in the room. "Don't apologize! You guys had your hands full getting us out and dealing with the FBI. I am just glad that you didn't end up hurt too!"

Johanna replied, "Ahiga is waiting at home to see you after awhile. We should let you rest and visit with your parents. I just wanted to make sure that you were okay."

"Thank-you. I'll be better once these wires are out of me," I laughed and waved her off.

We turned on the tv to old reruns of "I Love Lucy" which had always made the two of us laugh. Since I was the only girl around, mom always enjoyed being able to watch some of her guilty pleasures with me. Dad brought us in some water and smuggled in some hospital contraband, chips. He knew our favorite so well which were ranch flavored Doritos. Eating them were a tad bit difficult with an IV stuck in my hand, but I managed. Looking over I saw Atsa start to fall asleep and wondered why no one had come to visit him. I didn't really know him that well at all if I didn't know he was all alone. I needed to remedy that soon.

Chapter 27

The next morning, I was awoken again by a knocking at my hospital door. I was expecting the FBI since I am sure they wanted to wrap things up, however it was a tall doctor wearing a white coat and his stethoscope. A sweet-faced nurse followed in after him. They came over to check out my vitals and then checked on Atsa.

Afterwards the doctor sat on one of those rolling chairs and pulled up next to me and my mom with his clipboard in hand. He rattled off a list of things wrong with me and what they had given me along with procedures performed. Neither mom or I really understood all the medical terms, but I did understand when he said, "You are healing nicely and there don't seem to be any complications. Just make sure to take it easy, stay hydrated, and if any of your stitches get infected go to the hospital immediately. Other than that, you are free to go and will be discharged."

"What about Atsa?" I asked.

"We will discharge your friend too, but he needs someone to take care of him and help him out. Don't be too hard on him," he advised me with a somewhat stern look.

Right as he was walking out of the room, the FBI agent, Detective Natalya, knocked to come in. The doctor grumbled under his breath about patients never getting any help. She said, "Now that you are discharged we have a van downstairs and we are going out to the dig to solve this. If it gets too hard let us know. We are going to wheel you out to the van to prevent any extra exertion for now."

With that several nurses came in to help us get unhooked from the hospital machines and get us placed gently in the wheelchairs. Then they wheeled down through the elevators and out to the van. As we went out the doors I whispered conspiratorially to Atsa, "It's like we are on a jailbreak!"

He smiled and whispered back, "Way to look at the bright side."

I hobbled from my wheelchair to the van door and slide in beside Zoe. I had been hoping to talk to her more yesterday, and the long ride through the desert seemed like the perfect opportunity. This van was quite a bit fancier than the dig's van. I felt like a spy slipping into the black surveillance type of van with blacked out windows. The cool air conditioning and smell of leather was a welcome change over the body odor and stale cigarette scent of our typical transportation.

Once seated I buckled my seatbelt which was another welcome change. Ya safety! Detective Natalya slid in and started up the van after she helped Atsa in and we were off. It didn't take long for us to be out of town and away from buildings. I turned to Zoe and said, "I follow you on Instagram, but I had no idea that you knew anything about me. Did you come out here on purpose or do you work with the FBI occasionally?"

"Yes and no," she answered carefully, "I do help out, but in this case I had seen your latest updates and knew something was wrong. I called Ezra and sure enough he found some suspicious clues and we decided to come out and help. Unfortunately, my intuition was a bit late and we couldn't save your from Nikkoli, but we can still help put the rest of the case to rest."

With that she turned and looked out the window. Ezra met my gaze in the mirror and shrugged, then indicated that the scenery was beautiful. After being shot at while hiking up steep rocks and falling down gravelly paths, I had lost sight of the beauty of the desert. The other day I had been worried that it would kill me now today the desert was a kaleidoscope of browns, reds, and yellows. I suppose it was hard to see the area around as beautiful when there was a madman trying to kill you and I could see why Zoe wanted to zone out and enjoy the passing colors.

As we were driving I saw a hawk cutting through the deep blue sky like a knife and wondered when and if I would be able to do that again. I felt a hand on my shoulder and saw that Atsa had been watching me closely. His gaze told me that we would enjoy a flight soon enough.

I could tell the moment we left the paved road and continued along the gravel path. It wouldn't be long until we reached the dig site. I turned in my seat and saw that my parents were following behind us. They must be worried how today would go and I was glad that they would be nearby.

With a screech of the brakes we pulled into the parking space. It felt strange not to be surrounded by the other interns. There would be no digging today and it was an eerily quiet as a graveyard. Half of the dig site had already been dug up while some was plotted to be started once the other grids had been cleared. It looked like an abandoned colony on the moon or a child's sandbox after they had grown too old to use it.

Everyone got out of the vehicles and we walked towards the edge, all looking to the distance for answers. That's when the detective turned to Zoe, "Are you ready? You start walking and tell us what you feel as we go around." She nodded and took a deep breath, then stepped forward. Seeming to follow a pathway that was only visible to her she stepped left, then right, a few further ahead. I could see her face twisted and whatever she was seeing it was not pleasant. I stepped closer to touch her hand and tell her it was okay, but Ezra stepped from behind and grabbed my arm. He shushed me and shook his head indicating that it must break the spell or something.

The hawk from before was now circling the area where Zoe was walking towards. Quietly, we trailed her from a short distance. When she finally stopped and sank to the ground. Her face a torrent of emotions. Her eyes flashed both anger and sadness, yet she looked afraid as well. On her knees now she started to claw at the dirt with her hands and that was when Ezra ran up and grabbed her breaking the spell. I could see the tears streaming down her face with gobs of mascara making her look like a frightful clown. I knew in that moment that she had seen more of my parents' last moments on Earth than I wanted to know.

Behind me I heard Detective Natalya walk up with a camera in one hand and a shovel in the other. My parents and Atsa both moved closer to me when they realized why the shovel was needed. I heard the crunch of the dirt beneath the shovel as she started digging and I couldn't help shedding a tear as they all hugged me. Over and over I heard the sound of crunching gravel and the thump it made as it was tossed aside. Wiping my eyes, I made myself look up from Atsa's tear soaked shirt and at the edge of the dig site I saw Lina. She seemed paler and sad, yet she had a small smile on her face. I wanted to run to her, but I couldn't.

Finally, after what seemed hours the detective dug deep enough to reveal two skeletons. She stepped back and took some crime scene photos, then stepped closer to examine the bodies. One had a turquoise pendant and a ring that had "with all my love, Clay" inscribed in the band and the other had a worn baseball camp I recognized from pictures. It was an awful way to see our parents especially for the first time that I could remember.

With wet eyes I looked up from the hastily dug grave and saw Lina wave at me before blowing me a kiss. Then she faded and in her place was a hawk who flew off into the setting sun. I watched until the image faded into the distance and I waved back. I turned back towards the group and realized no one else could see what I had just witnessed, but I knew that everything was going to be okay now. I just had that feeling.

About the Author

R.L. Walker is from Lithopolis, Ohio who loved reading from a young age and could often be found curled up with a book. I grew up in the carnival business before pursuing a degree in Anthropology and Archaeology from the University of South Florida. Parts of this book were inspired by time spent in a field school in Antigua and work in museums.

After graduation I found a job teaching English in South Korea where I spent a lot of time traveling Asia and dreaming up stories. Upon my return, I got my Masters in Education from Ohio University and started teaching writing to 5th and 6th graders at Allen Elementary in Chillicothe, Ohio. I used my own writing and struggles with the writing process to help motivate my students to write more and put their all into their work. After writing my first book, The Disappearing Act, which is a mystery set in the carnival I decided to keep writing.

I wanted to write another book in the series, but I was also concerned with the issues around the pipeline out West and wanted to create a story that would perhaps embellish on the ideas while shedding light on the larger issue. That people were losing their heritage for a profit.

I hope you enjoyed this book and would ask you to leave a review, good, bad, or ugly!

71746063R00102

Made in the USA
Middletown, DE
29 April 2018